COPPER & COBALT

Copper
and
Cobalt

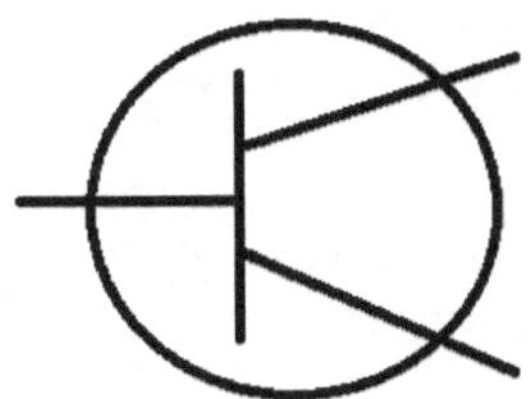

JESSICA D. COPLEN

The Periodic Tales
of Minni the Witch

Copper and Gold

Copper and Cobalt

Copper and Mercury

Copper and Palladium

For

The Coven

&

Sleepy Matilda

ONE[1]

I'm going to say this was my fault, sorta, mostly. Depends on who you ask. To be honest, I kind of lost track. I'm pretty sure I passed culpability somewhere between not calling 911 and kidnapping a member of the British monarchy.

At least this time we didn't lose Delaware.

You know what, don't worry about that. It's not important right now.

So, I guess it all started on Friday because apparently I can't do Fridays. I didn't go home for the holiday because we don't celebrate Thanksgiving in the Masterson household. I suppose I could have went anyway since I had the two days off. But Marcel had to work because he drew the short straw, and I thought I'd hang out with him so he wouldn't suffer alone. I saw him off to work, then went back to bed for like another hour before actually getting up.

Oh, Marcel's my boyfriend. Doesn't know anything about magic, and I like it that way. Well, I think it's better that way. We had a bit of a rough patch two months ago, but we worked through it. However, the topic of co-habitation is still taboo.

I'd stayed over at his place the night before, and yes, I do have a whole drawer full of clean clothes there. Yes, I stole one of his Yale t-shirts. It's not really stealing though, right? I mean, they smell just like him, and by that I mean they smell like new pennies. Which is weird, I know, but I don't care. I like it.

Yeah, I can ramble sometimes, especially after a trauma, so feel free to nudge me if I start to get off track. You can call me Minni by the way, instead of Dominique. Everyone else does.

Right, so, I had plans for Friday: errands to run, that kind of thing. I grabbed my coat, my laptop bag, and headed to Phil's store, The Mercury Shop, over in Brooklyn. Since magic users don't really live in big cities because our magic wreaks havoc on technology—stupid TechnoMages—The Mercury Shop is a place for magic users to go where they can be safe should they accidently end up in New York City. It happens, you know. The wrong spell, the wrong turn in the Shadow Realm; you never know where you might end up.

Phil sells practical magic supplies for creating potions and stuff. But he pays the bills (and keeps suspicion off himself) by selling actual stuff you might find in a 'trendy book store,' minus the overpriced lattes. On the left side of the store is all manner of crafts, from dried herbs to crystals to things I'm not entirely sure what they are but I am sure they're responsible for the musky layer of incense that constantly fills the room.

To the right is a wall of shelves with all kinds of books on magic, lore, religion, you name it. Some of it you could find easily online, but there is a fair amount of older and harder to locate stuff that keeps the true believers coming back. If you're a wizard who has Phil's trust, he'll let you shop on the third floor where he keeps the heavy stuff. Phil's had several collections from older wizards bequeathed to him over the years and he promised he would only give the books to good homes.

He's never let me have one. I'm okay with this.

Oh, Phil is our local coven leader. He watches over the few wizards that live in New York City. He's a good friend, like an older brother or maybe a second cousin. He's also my warden, but that's an even longer story and did I mention I ramble?

When I got to Phil's shop he was ringing out a customer at the register. I pretended to browse the herb section to see how many I could recognize without looking at the label. This I'm surprisingly good at. It helps that I grew up on a farm in Nebraska and have a younger sister who is wicked amazing at potions and spellcraft. I always thought being really good at herbal magic is like being a four-star chef, only when Gordan Ramsey yells at you, his comments are less figurative and more literal.

This meat is so raw its entrails can be used to tell the future!

"Do you grow your own supplies?" the lady at the counter asked Phil as he handed her back her change.

"No," he was polite. "It's all organically grown upstate."

"I have family in the Catskills. It's quite lovely up there." The woman was in no hurry to take her purchase and leave, slowly folding her money into her wallet which she had taken forever to dig out of her purse.

"I'll have to take your word for it." Phil gave her an awkward smile. The woman wasn't a wizard, not even a Forsaken.

"You have a really great shop here," she continued to chat up Phil who was staring blankly at her, though in a polite way.

"Thank you." Phil started to randomly straighten things on the counter.

"Hey, shop keep," I laid my Nebraskan accent on thick. "Got any of that rosemary and thyme?" And yeah, I purposely mispronounced thyme.

"Individual or mixed?" Phil moved from behind the counter and started to head over.

"What's the difference?" I played dumb, my accent is good for that. People tend to think intelligence is directly disproportioned to the way someone speaks. What a load of hooey. "Aren't they the same thing?"

Phil's back was to the woman and he allowed himself a bemuse smirk before he started to comment on the general and mystical properties of the two herbs. The lady got the hint and took her purchases, waving goodbye as she left. Once she was outside and clear of the front glass display, Phil relaxed.

"Thank you for that." He put back the bottle of crushed rosemary leaves he had grabbed for effect.

"You could just tell her you're not interested?" I suggested.

"She spends entirely too much on tea."

"How very capitalist of you," I replied drolly.

"Speaking of." Phil gestured to the counter.

Now, Phil's shop is chock full of magic and anyone not in the know kind of hates the place because they can never get a signal on their phone. Using magic creates this static that messes with anything that's got a circuit board in it. Magic basically turns wizards into walking electromagnets, without the fun sticking to things. And you knew that. Sorry.

So, I have a personal sigil: a circle with a line offset down the middle, three lines coming from outside the circle to touch the center line. It's a simplified diagram of a transistor. I've carved it into every electrical item I own so if I use magic or go into a high magic area, like Phil's shop, then all the static is filtered away. It also translates that magical energy into electrical energy which keeps my batteries from dying. My electricity bill is so freaking low, it's ridiculous. Awesome, but ridiculous.

I can do this because, well, energy is what I do.

Phil cleared off a space on the counter as I pulled my laptop from my bag. Since Phil couldn't have a computer, he borrows mine from time to time. I opened up a wifi hotspot on my phone, managed to get a signal, and let him at it. About once a month I go by the shop and let Phil use the laptop for work stuff. There are a few non-magical companies that he can only order from or pay online. We count this as checking in with my parole officer time.

"Always appreciated," Phil said. He grabbed a notepad from under his cash register which, I kid you not, came out of an old General Store someplace west of Oklahoma City. It was all mechanical, really cool looking, but it makes keeping inventory and receipts a bit of a pain.

"Happy to be of service." I gave him a mock salute.

Phil just rolled his eyes then went about his business. Oh my god, he is such a horribly slow typer.

I drummed my fingers on the countertop. "So, I'm thinking you can buy me lunch at that little bistro two blocks over. I know you love that monstrosity they make."

He made a face at me, pressing his lips together and crinkling his nose. "You think anything with sprouts is a monstrosity."

"Yeah." Duh.

Phil chuckled and tapped at the keys. "Sounds good. Ryan can watch the store, I'll bring something back for him."

"Where is Ryan?" I asked, grabbing my phone so I could text Stacey, she's my non-magical BFF, about plans for later that weekend.

"Upstairs, cataloguing some stuff," Phil answered, then looked towards the door as the little bell dinged announcing a new customer. "Welcome."

I was in the middle of my text, totally ignoring my surroundings—which is why I would make a horrible spy—when I saw Phil rush around the counter. At that same moment I heard the clatter of one of the display tables being knocked over. Glancing up, I saw the powder blue-clad figure of a man slumped on the floor, Phil rushing to his side.

"Should I call 911?" I said as I hurried over, wondering if maybe the person only tripped and knocked down the display.

Phil leaned over the collapsed man, who looked to be in his late forties, maybe early fifties. The clamminess of his skin and generally sunken appearance made it hard to tell. He looked sick, like plague-carrier sick.

"I'm gonna call 911." I clicked out of texting to get to the dialing keypad.

"Wait." Phil had one hand held over the man's face while the other hovered over the general region where the heart should be. I had only gotten the 9 dialed so I paused, trusting my coven leader, because I tell you, this guy looked like he was about to die at any second.

"Ryan!" Phil shouted at the top of his lungs as he started to clear away the fallen boxes of soap the stranger had taken down with him.

Loud thuds preceded Ryan running out of the back room, skidding to a stop, a little wide-eyed, at the scene.

"I need all the Prussian Blue we have in the store," Phil ordered and Ryan only paused for a second before disappearing into the back again. "Help me move him."

Realizing he was talking to me, I pocketed my phone and

grabbed the man's legs as Phil reached up under the arms. Together we carried the guy into the back where Phil had a makeshift breakroom complete with battered leather sofa.

We laid the guy on the sofa, then Phil immediately moved to the shelf where he keeps his office supplies. You know, the usual: pens, sticky-notes, highlighters, exorcism kit...

"Get his tie off," he told me as he rummaged through one of the boxes. "Help him breath."

"Uh, okay." I still had no clue what was going on but hey, sounded reasonable to me. I watch a lot of movies.

Trying not to be too rough, I tugged at the tie, getting it loose enough to just slip it out of its knot and from around his neck. I also undid the first two buttons on his dress shirt. I grabbed a random hoodie that lay over the back of a nearby chair and folded it up to make a pillow. I didn't want to really tilt his head up, just make it lay more even with his body.

I made the stranger about as comfortable as I could. As I started to turn back to Phil, I felt a cold grip on my arm.

"*Seren cobalt.*" The man stared at me with vacant, glassed over eyes.

"Seh-ren cobalt?" Pretty sure that's what he said.

His eyes rolled into the back of his head as he passed out again, his grip loosening and his arm falling from the sofa.

Great. See? This is how horror movies start.

TWO²

"Are you sure I shouldn't be calling 911?" There was some Grade-A M. Night crap going on here.

"They won't be able to help him." Phil was putting a mortar and pestle on the table along with a large semi-gilded book which he started flipping through. "I think he's got heavy metal poisoning."

"What, like mercury?"

Ryan came down the back stairwell with a couple of bottles in his hands. "This is all we have."

Phil glanced at the labels before taking one and carefully pouring the contents into the mortar. "I'm thinking either cesium or thallium."

"Then I should call 911." I'm not that familiar with heavy metal poisoning in general, but I do know that too much mercury turns you bat shit crazy. Thank you, Mad Hatter.

"Won't do any good." Phil grabbed a second bottle which contained a bright blue powder, like someone had crushed a bunch of chalk. "The poison has been magically enhanced."

"Right, okay, ix-nay on the ine-one-one-nay." When you magically enhance something poisonous, the only way to combat it is with magic... or magically enhanced medicines.

You know, I find it interesting how many herbs and natural organic compounds have scientifically measurable properties that are basically magic. I mean, magic is just really advanced physics. Throw a little biochemistry in there and you can unlock so much lost potential. It's all about being able to effect the very nature of the substance of the universe. Or at least asking it nicely to do your bidding.

Except magic isn't an exact science...

But there's enough wiggle room to increase or decrease the potency of a herb or drug. This can be as simple as effecting the absorption rate or as complicated as making it attack only certain genetic markers. And basic herbal magic can be done by anyone, even me. Okay maybe not me.

If you want to really start messing around with herbs then ideally you should be as learned as a real physician. And if you want to fight a poison that's been mucked with, then you'll have to do some tampering of your own with the cure.

"Get me some garlic heads from the front." Phil ordered absently.

"On it." I wasn't sure if he was talking to me or Ryan but occasionally I feel the need to be useful.

I went to the herbal section at the front of the store and grabbed a bushel of garlic heads. I then realized that maybe it wasn't a good time for more random strangers to walk in. I went over to the door and slid the deadbolt. Phil's security is classy like that, I then turned around the "Open" sign so it said "Closed."

A flicker of energy ran through the building, humming outside of most people's perspective. Phil's wards strengthened in response to the building being closed. It was a neat trick and better than any alarm system.

Well, Phil has an alarm system for insurance purposes, but it's fried.

I was about to turn away when I saw two small figures standing ominously across the road. And by ominously, I mean I could have just been imagining the whole thing. Turns out I wasn't, but at the time I couldn't be sure if I was just being paranoid. They weren't there at the second glance. After a quick scan of the street, I decided to trust in the wards and headed into the back room.

Philhad poured a touch of milk into the mortar and the room was starting to smell a little rank. That's another fun thing about magic: all the new and exciting smells it creates. One of these days I'm going to create a spell that just smells of cotton candy. Not sure what it'll do, but it will smell delicious!

Tearing into one of the garlic heads, I set the cloves down next to him. "What you making?"

"A cure, hopefully." He grabbed a nearby spoon and went to town on the garlic, smooshing up a few cloves before tossing them into the mortar. "I need you to message Ricard. I've got my hands full."

"Kay," I said and grabbed Phil's sender from his desk in the corner. Ricard is a magic healer that lives in upstate New York. He's basically the equivalent of a PhD surgeon while Phil is more of an EMT. "What do you want me to say, exactly?"

"Tell him I'm treating a patient who has magically induced acute heavy metal poisoning with a Dunkelblau Colloidal," Phil dictated. I wrote it down word for word, sending it off to Ricard. In theory, Ricard or one of his apprentices would see it right away.

"Got it," Ryan said. He started to rummage through a wallet. It took me a moment to realize where it came from.

"Did you just pickpocket a dying man?" I wasn't nearly as disgusted with the idea as I probably should have been.

"Yes." And apparently neither was Ryan. "His name is Rodney Perkins, of Dover, Delaware."

Both Phil and I paused and looked at each other.

"Please tell me that is a coincidence," I asked Phil.

"Me saying it doesn't make it true." Phil frowned then went back to his work, starting to mutter in Latin.

"You know this guy?" Ryan asked.

"No." I thought back to September. "Remember when we broke into the Cloisters to stop Clint Canton and we ended up fighting a gold dragon?"

"Doesn't ring a bell," Ryan deadpanned.

I replied with an equally blank stare as Phil continued to muck about with his magic cure. I gave in pretty quickly, though. "When Canton was trying to open the rift between our world and the Shadow Realm, we interrupted the spell, but it still opened a small rift where his dagger fell."

"Let me guess." Ryan held up the ID. "Dover, Delaware?"

"It could just be a coincidence." I chewed on my lip and tried to think if there were any connections I missed. I turned to Phil. "What about the security guard, Dubins? What did he have to say?"

"Nothing that makes me think this man is connected to Clint," Phil admitted. "But it could be related the fact we opened a portal to the Shadow Realm there."

"Hey, that was Drake's fault." It was! He was being such a d-bag!

Phil's sender glowed and I read the return message aloud. "Ricard is currently in surgery. He advised to continue with treatment and notify him immediately if the patient has a negative reaction."

Phil nodded and added some distilled vinegar to the mix.

Ryan was still rummaging through Perkins's wallet. "Looks like he works at Delaware State University. That's what, three hours away?"

He handed me a faculty ID card which didn't do more than show what Perkins looked like when not deathly ill, and perhaps ten years younger. I used my phone to pull up the DSU website and searched for Perkins. "It says here he's an environmental scientist in the Department of Agriculture and Natural Resources."

"That sounds entirely too boring to be worth poisoning the guy over."

"Yeah," I agreed. There was a slight pop and sizzle. I turned to see blue smoke rising from Phil's mortar. "Is it supposed to do that?"

"Yes." Phil grabbed a mug and strained the contents of the mortar into it. It looked like gritty, pure-blue ink. "Sit Mr. Perkins up. He'll have to drink this."

"I don't think he can do much of anything right now," I mumbled as I moved over to the sofa to prop up Perkins, who was barely responsive. As I held Perkins's head, Ryan pinched his nose while Phil force fed him the concoction.

"Watch the shirt!" There was much spillage, Ryan jumping

back as far as he could, afraid of getting the blue liquid on his t-shirt. It's for this band no one has ever heard of, called Purgatory. Ryan loves them so much and makes me take him to their concerts every time they're in town.

Phil and I gave him a synchronized eye-roll and continued to force-feed Perkins. If the stuff worked, then it worked. The poison would be counter-acted and would no longer hurt him. However, his body needed to recover and repair whatever damage was done. We could have tried casting another spell to speed recovery, but sometimes it's just best to let nature do its thing. The more you pile magic spells on top of each other, the more likely it's all going to come tumbling down like a bad game of Jenga.

"What's in this by the way?" I asked after wiping up some of the blue liquid from Perkins's neck and chin.

"Basically, it's a charcoal and Prussian Blue solution with a heavy dose of anti-magic." Phil cleaned up his mess on the table, a light frown on his face.

"Prussian Blue." I knew that term. I can't remember from where. "Isn't that paint?"

"It's a color pigment, yes." Phil walked into the small bathroom to wash the mortar out in the sink. "But it's a potassium ferric ferrocyanide."

"You say those words like they're real," said Ryan.

"Medical Prussian Blue is used to combat heavy metal poisoning."

"And you just happen to have medical grade Prussian Blue?" I asked, but it didn't really surprise me.

"Eh, close enough." He returned the mortar to the table. "If it was a straight up poisoning, then it might not have been the best idea."

"But it was magical poisoning." Ryan snooped through Phil's book. Though I don't think it counts as snooping if Phil wouldn't really care.

Phil scratched his head. "I don't know yet if someone used magic to give him the poison, or if the poison was magically enhanced and given to him normally."

"How much difference could that make?" I asked.

"Not really sure." Phil tugged at his book to get it away from Ryan. "We'll just have to see how he reacts in the next few hours."

"Guess that scraps lunch then."

"You'll just have to get it to go," Phil replied, completely ignoring the fact I wasn't being serious. "I'm going to need more Prussian Blue. I have some at my apartment. Would you go fetch it and grab lunch on the way back?"

Phil's apartment wasn't too terribly far; I could easily walk there and back, swinging around to stop at the restaurant on the way. "Sounds good. Oh, Perkins said something earlier but I'm not sure it was English. *Seren cobalt*."

"Are you sure you're pronouncing that correctly?" Phil frowned at me.

"Pretty sure." I know my Nebraskan accent has softened over the past few years but apparently I still can't say words like 'wash' and 'pecan' correctly. At least I stopped pluralizing everything. "Do you know what it means?"

"Well, cobalt sounds like cobalt." Phil got that little crinkle between his eyes. "I'm not sure about the other one. I could try a translation spell."

Ryan held up his hand. "Don't you have an app for this?"

Yeah, sometimes I forget technology can be handier than magic—stupid TechnoMages. I pulled up a translation app and said the words as clearly as possible. It took a few tries to get my Midwestern mouth to form the correct sounds, but I got there in the end.

Language: Welsh
Native: seren cobalt
Translation: star cobalt; the Cobalt Star
Yeah, not helpful.

THREE[3]

"The Cobalt Star—why does that sound familiar?" Phil asked, though I don't believe he was expecting a legitimate answer.

"Because you're a magic encyclopedia?" That's generally the answer to those kinds of questions.

"I foresee much research in my future," Ryan spoke with a charlatan's voice.

After a little more discussion, it was decided I'd go fetch the pigment and grab some food. Pinky and the Brain would crack open the reference materials while keeping an eye on Perkins. We hadn't a clue as to why someone would try to poison the man, nor why he would have come to Phil's shop. I mean, did Perkins go to Phil's because he was magically poisoned and needed help? Or was he poisoned because someone knew he was going to Phil's?

Our only clue, other than the strange Dover, Delaware coincidence, was the mysteriously Welsh Cobalt Star.

I walked to Phil's apartment without incident. His wards were at full strength since he wasn't home, but they were programmed to basically ignore me as long as I wasn't under any undue influence. I found the stash of Prussian Blue where he said it would be, in the kitchen, middle cabinet, behind the Wool of Bat.

I can't believe he still had that...

My plan was to stop at the bistro on the way back to pick up the order I called in. It was a decent plan, I thought. And I was making good time. I tend to walk fast as I'm bit of a running junkie. It was near lunchtime so it was nice outside, bright and warm—comparatively speaking. It's November in New York but hey, global warming.

Anyway, I started to get that eerie feeling like I was being watched. Not in the magical sense, but in the literal, which is a lot more disconcerting I tell you. The little hairs stick up, your body becomes hypersensitive, adrenaline starts to pump...

At first I tried to use the shop windows to scope out who might be following me, keeping my pace as steady and normal as possible. There wasn't a single suspicious person, which is kinda strange in and of itself. No one was bothering to even look at me for more than a passing glance. I got to thinking that maybe I was just being paranoid, but it's only paranoia if you don't actually end up getting used as a bowling ball by a dragon... Sorry, I'm still not over that.

Yeah, it was a thing that happened.

I don't want to talk about it.

Waiting my turn at a stop light, I still couldn't shake the feeling. So I did what any sensible person would do: I ran through the intersection, dodging a Tahoe and at least two Prius.

I'm sorry, I should have put a negative modifier in there somewhere...

The move went noticed by a few people who bothered to shout at me that I'm an idiot—which, thanks, I know—but no one followed me. I jogged down the sidewalk to put as much distance as I could between myself and whoever it was that was watching me. I had to hold my courier bag against my stomach to keep it from flopping around. The Prussian Blue was in a glass container and I really didn't want to break it.

But the feeling that I was being watched wouldn't go away. It didn't even taper down.

I was coming up on a bus shelter and in the reflection of the plastic I saw two dark shapes, both vaguely human, who floated about five feet off the ground behind me.

I've seen this movie... It does not end well for me.

Booking it, I ran down the sidewalk, dodging all the random people, before I saw something that made me feel strangely safe. Making a hard left, I nearly crashed through the glass door. I pulled it open and darted inside. I then grabbed the handle and tugged against the hydraulics to close it.

Looking outside, the dark figures were nowhere to be seen. I hoped that didn't mean they were right behind me. I again got the feeling I was being watched, but this time it was in that socially awkward sense.

Clearing my throat, I turned around and tried to compose myself as I surveyed the room. The place was decently busy, only those nearest the door really noticed my panicked entrance. After a moment they shook their heads and went back to whatever it was they'd been doing.

So yeah, I decided to hide out in a Dunkin' Donuts. I even ordered a coffee.

Decaf…

Don't judge me.

"And you're sure you were being followed?" Phil asked over a decently stable connection. He has an older, corded style phone that doesn't have a lot of electronics. It wouldn't last much longer, though.

"Pretty darn sure." I had snagged a corner of the Dunkin' Donuts where I could see both the front entrance and the hallway into the back. "I know I can get a little paranoid at times, but I'm not making this up."

"I trust you." He had a bit of a 'hrm' tone to his voice. "Dark floating figures… That could be a number of things."

"Maybe something from the Welsh tradition?"

"That doesn't really narrow it down," he said. One of the largest wellsprings of magic resides in Wales. It's impossible to throw a rock there without hitting something magical. "I called Harper," Phil continued. "He's on his way over. I'll have him pick you up."

"Harper?" He's this police detective who helped us when an ancient gold dragon had been kidnapped by an emotionally traumatized wizard trying to destroy the world, or maybe just Manhattan. The Delaware incident I mentioned earlier, opening a riff in Dover, was the result of our first failed attempt to rescue the dragon. "Isn't he out of the 34th precinct?"

"Brooklyn is definitely out of his jurisdiction," Phil agreed. "I needed someone to run background on Perkins. I figure if this is related to Dover then it would be better to have someone who is already familiar with what happened."

"Good idea." This is why Phil is coven leader.

A little bit later I got a text from Harper telling me he was on his way. Considering New York traffic, I guestimated an ETA and called the bistro I ordered lunch from to tell them I'd be late. I was extremely polite because if I've learned anything over the last few years is that a) there's no such thing as a good vampire, b) never invade Russia in winter, and c) don't piss off the people who handle your food.

Harper made good time, I think he used his sirens at one point because he was in a police cruiser instead of his personal vehicle. He double-parked and didn't bother getting out of the car.

Trying not to look like a complete idiot, I checked every angle I could see before slowly opening the door to the Dunkin's. Left, right, up, down, I didn't see the dark figures or anyone looking at me suspiciously. Well, the street food vendor a few feet down gave me a 'don't make eye contact with the crazy lady' glance before going back to turning his sausages.

Taking no chances, I darted out through the parked vehicles and climbed into the cruiser, closed the door swiftly, and hit the lock.

"You alright?" Harper asked as I put on my seatbelt.

"Oh, I'm just dandy," I replied as I got myself situated, gently pushing my bag into the floorboard while pulling out a small paper sack. "Munchkin?"

The cop gave me an unamused look. "Really, donuts?"

"Munchkins," I corrected him, opening up the sack so he could see the donut rounds which, okay, yeah fine, they're donut adjacent.

"Ah, what the hell." Harper gave in and grabbed one, chewing on it as he pulled out into traffic.

Harper is a pretty cool guy. He's the grandson of Nigerian immigrants and he's a Forsaken. He has the ability to use magic, but doesn't, so he only has a small magical static field. And since he knows the truth about magic, he can help us out when the truth becomes stranger than fiction.

We didn't have very far to go. I'd been planning on walking the whole way. When we got to the bistro, Harper double parked again. This time he went in and got the food, leaving me safe in a locked police cruiser. I know, sounds crazy, taking the time to stop for sandwiches when there was a guy laying comatose on Phil's sofa and I'm being stalked by floating dark shadowy thingies.

But, to be honest, I've had worst days, and Perkins was stable, so... Food.

Harper didn't feel like repeating himself so he held off on what he knew about Perkins until we got to Phil's. Harper parked in the alley and exited the vehicle first, gun drawn but kept low. Then, when he thought it was safe, he rushed me inside.

Here at Phillip McCree's Mercury Shop we take our paranoia very seriously.

"Food!" Ryan started to rummage through the take-out sack. See, I'm not the only one who has their priorities straight.

As Ryan passed out the sandwiches, Harper filled us in on what he managed to discover about our comatose friend. "Rodney Perkins, emigrated from Wales sixteen years ago, but started at DSU seven years ago. No criminal record, unless you count one speeding ticket."

Phil frowned. "If he emigrated from Wales, then there goes all our theories about the Cobalt Star."

"What do you mean?" I think that's what Ryan said. His mouth was full of pastrami on rye.

"Perkins is out of it," I explained because I was kind of proud of myself for figuring it out on my own. "We can't be sure he spoke Welsh because the Cobalt Star is Welsh or because his mind decided to use his native Welsh instead of English in his confused state."

"Oh." Ryan nodded. "Like when you get tired you start sounding like the mumbling guy, ah, Jeff, from *King of the Hill*?"

I was not amused. Even if it was true. I never should have told Ryan he could come over and watch television when I'm out.

"Mr. Perkins does have a car registered to him," Harper continued, expertly ignoring us. "A light blue Chevy Cobalt."

"Do you think he named his car Star?" Ryan offered.

"He's dying and he mumbles about his car?" I know I have my priorities all screwed up, but this guy?

"He must have drove," Phil concluded. "He didn't have anything on him like a bus ticket and a ride share would have been way too expensive, I would think."

"But he also didn't have any keys," Ryan pointed out. He would know, seeing as he pick-pocketed the man.

Harper let out a long sigh. "Well, he either drove or he didn't. If he did then his car has to be parked around here somewhere."

I slapped my hands together. "We should probably go look for it then."

"Whatever's following you is still out there," Harper quickly pointed out.

"Which is why you shouldn't go out there alone either, cop or not." I've seen enough horror movies to understand the need for safety in numbers. I really should have thought of that earlier.

"You might also be looking for something magical," Phil added as he started to gather the ingredients for another batch of Prussian Blue antidote. "It could be something you might not be able to see. One of us should go with you, and I'm afraid Minni is the best choice."

I kind of scrunched up my face. "You're *afraid* I'm the best choice?"

Phil gave me a semi-apologetic frown. "If you get attacked, you have the best defense. Plus, depending on what you saw, you're already tagged. No need to let them know about me and Ryan if they don't already."

"I'm going to agree with everything you said, but I reserve the right to be insulted."

"Sure."

"Right. Shall we go?" Harper gestured towards the front.

"We can check the lot down the block," I said helpfully. "That's where most people park."

"Good idea," Phil replied. "Be careful."

"Of course." I nodded and headed to the front with Harper and Ryan.

Ryan let us out, then locked the door, saying through the glass, "Don't die."

Yeah... that was kind of the plan.

Looking for Perkins's car, and watching for whatever had been chasing me, we both made swift strides down the street. I kept checking the glass and reflective surfaces. Sometimes magical beings can't be seen directly.

"Hold up." Harper held his arm out and stopped me, my heart doing a bit of a thump-badump. He scooped down and picked up a set of keys that lay in the grating of a planted tree.

"DSU." I pointed at the keychain which bore the initials and colors of the university. Perkins must have dropped them as the poison kicked in. It was a miracle they were still there.

With a nod, we kept going, watching out for anything else that could have been dropped. Other than the usual junk, there was no sign of Perkins or the shadowy things I saw.

We reached the parking lot which was one of those pay-to-park types. It could probably hold forty cars and looked pretty packed. It was easy enough to spot the light blue Cobalt with out-of-state plates on the second row.

"Wait." It was my turn to stop Harper. "Gimme the keys."

"Okay." Harper raised a brow at me but handed them over.

I grabbed his arm and moved to stand behind a SUV. Once we were out of the line of fire, I pointed the fob at the Cobalt. The fob, you know, the remote thingy. It's a fob. I'm calling it a fob, so it's a fob.

Anyway... I pointed the *fob* at the car and hit unlock.

The lights blinked.

"You thought it might explode?" Harper had an amused grin on his face, that one eyebrow cocked slightly.

"Maybe? Oh come on, it was a possibility." Hey, Perkins was drugged with something like thallium. I've had time to Google that stuff and it's all very cloak and dagger-y, you know?

"Well, if it will make you feel better." Harper got down on the ground next to the Cobalt and proceeded to check the undercarriage. "Yep, that's a really big bomb, bunch of blinky lights, and oh, a blue wire!"

"You're hilarious and I'm very annoyed I didn't think of that joke first." I looked in the backseat. "Hey, a briefcase."

"You check it," Harper said as he stood, dusting the dirt off his trousers. "I'm gonna check the trunk."

"Do we need gloves?" I asked as I handed him the keys.

"I get the feeling none of this is going to make it into an actual police report." He headed behind the car. "Magical thallium poisoning cured by equally magical blue ink? Not sure how I'd even start to explain that one."

"Right." Couldn't really argue with him there. I opened the rear driver's side door, the briefcase sitting in the floorboard. I grabbed it and placed it on the seat. I frowned at the three-number tumblers next to both catches. "Please don't be locked."

I suck at Entropy magic by the way. Both of the locks wouldn't budge. With a grumble I pushed it away and started looking around for anything else that might be of help.

Climbing between the seats, I sat down in the passenger's side. "Found his phone!" I called to Harper as I picked it up. "Battery's dead."

That was a bust, so I turned my attention to the glove box. Nothing particular exciting there either: insurance papers, the last few oil change receipts, a bunch of napkins. I did notice an empty bottle of orange juice in the floorboard next to a Nutter Butter wrapper.

Taking one of the handy napkins, I used it to pick up the bottle. Harper might not be too worried about the evidence from an overall standpoint, but if the bottle was what I thought it was, it may be the only piece evidence worth preserving.

I held it up to the light and focused my Third Eye to see

the item in the metaphysical world.

"The trunk was a wash." Harper climbed into the backseat. "I take it the briefcase was locked?"

"Uh huh," I replied, though my focus wasn't really on him. "I think I found our murder weapon. Or, well, attempted murder weapon."

"Someone poisoned his orange juice?"

"I can sense the magical residue." I shook my head and cleared my vision. "Someone cast magic on the bottle and the contents."

Harper went into full on cop mode. "Depending on how potent the poison was and how long he took to drink it, it would explain why he didn't present with symptoms during his drive. Whoever poisoned him probably hoped he'd pass out, crash his car, and no one would be the wiser."

I frowned at him. "Wouldn't you guys check for this stuff?"

"Why?" The man shrugged his shoulders. "A heart attack while driving is a million times more likely than magical heavy metal poisoning. And most heavy metals aren't in the standard tests. We'd have to have cause to look for it."

Okay, he had me there. "Fair, but why not just make him have an actual heart attack?"

Harper looked up at me sharply, those detective eyes narrowing. "That's a thing?"

"Technically." I let out a nervous chuckle. "But it's all Black List spells."

Hey, I may be guilty of manslaughter, but I would never purposefully induce a heart attack in someone. Even if it would be totally easy because all I'd have to do is introduce a defibrillating electrical pulse and... And yeah, I may have thought about this way too much.

I sometimes get bored at project meetings, alright?

Thinking is not the same as doing.

It's called impulse control.

Oh, the manslaughter thing? Well, it was years ago and basically self-defense. It's another long story that isn't important right now.

"Any of these receipts for the orange juice?" Harper gestured to the random bits of paper.

"Ah..." That was a good question. I quickly scanned the few receipts that were in the pile of papers. "Doesn't look like it."

"Ryan say anything about Perkins having a store receipt on him?"

"Nope, and I didn't ask." I frowned as I put the bottle on the driver's seat. I should really learn to ask more questions.

"It would be nice to know when and where he picked this up." Harper pulled out his phone, checking something quickly before adding, "If Perkins bought this on the way up here, then someone was stalking him. If he brought it from home, that's even more insidious. I doubt I could get cause for a warrant to pull his credit card information."

"What if he paid by cash?" I realized the flaw.

"Won't know till we have a look." Harper grimaced. "I wonder if Phil knows any Forsaken cops down in Dover who can check out Mr. Perkins's house? Off the books."

"Ooo, that's a good idea."

"Sir," a stern baritone voice called out to us. "I'm gonna ask you to get out of the car, slowly, with your hands up."

Harper looked like he had just been told they were out of butter at the movie theater. We both glanced through the rear window to see a uniformed police officer standing a few feet back, hand resting on his holstered gun.

"You have got to be kidding me," Harper mumbled as he did what the man told him. I didn't know if the cop had seen me, so I just went as small I could.

"Officer," Harper said once he was standing outside the car with his hands up. "I'm Detective Laurence Harper out of the 34th Precinct, Manhattan."

Thankfully, Harper was wearing his badge on his belt, but the uniform didn't completely relax. "Got a call of suspicious characters messing around with some of the vehicles parked here, and that they were armed."

"That would be me." Harper slowly lowered his hands. "This vehicle, it's… It's part of an ongoing investigation."

Harper had left the rear driver's door open and I sat sideways on the front passenger's seat, trying to see what was going on without being seen myself. The two of them walked away from the car towards the uniformed officer's squad car. Harper was making up some story and I really hoped I wasn't going to be quizzed on it later.

I heard a bit of a squeaking noise and a huff of air, and I instinctively started to pump magic into my focus bracelet. My heart did that thump-badump thing again as I remembered the dark figures that had hovered behind me as I ran down the street earlier. Then I realized I was in a tight, confined space and shooting electricity, no matter how good with energy I am, probably isn't the smartest idea I could ever come up with.

That's when I saw it.

It had to have been maybe two feet tall, at the most, and so ugly that it came full circle until it was kind of cute. The little goblin-like creature had climbed up onto the seat and was working his way across. He had grossly exaggerated features, sharp pointed ears, and a long-angled nose. His hands were knobby and puffy, his skin the color of vomit. He wore a rather smart looking red sweater and brown pants. No shoes though, and he was in dire need of a pedicure.

He looked up at me with these milky blue eyes and shook himself in a startled manner, scuttling up against the back seat.

"Hey there," I tried to say as nicely as I could despite not knowing if the creature would respond violently.

He said something to me in what I thought was maybe German. I was completely clueless. So I continued to smile but tried not to bare my teeth too much. "English?"

He spoke again as he relaxed, moving forward slightly. I thought he switched languages, but I still didn't understand him. He started to ramble, his hands moving as if he was explaining something to me. At one point I swear he gave me the bitch face followed by what were probably curse words.

He looked back up at me with his milky eyes and I gave him an apologetic shrug. The little guy frowned at me. I guess he thought I'd be more sympathetic? Waving me off, the goblin moved back across the seat and grabbed a hold of the briefcase handle. He then started to drag it towards the open door.

"Hey, no." I grabbed the case. "That's evidence!"

Yeah, I don't think supernatural creatures care about proper police procedure. Not that I tend to either. Also I got there first.

I tugged at the briefcase,but the little guy was stronger than he looked. I moved forward, bracing myself as I tried to get a better grip. The goblin cursed at me (if his tone was anything to go by) and tried to wrench it from my grasp.

"Leggo!" I shouted as I nearly became wedged between the seats.

I heard a buzzing, kind of like a hummingbird if it was on Redbull, and two big birds came sweeping into the vehicle. At least that's what I thought they were at first, most of my attention being on the briefcase. When I glanced up, I was confronted by two very angry looking pixies. They were both wearing these dark blue and green gossamer dresses to match the colors of their butterfly-like wings.

One of them swooped down to attack the goblin while the other went after me. I let go of the briefcase with my right hand and brought it up to defend myself. The pixie latched onto my arm with its sharp but thankfully short talon-like nails. It was like being attacked by an angry house cat. Only probably less life threatening.

I reacted defensively, sending out an electrical shock from my focus bracelet. But the problem with reactive magic is that, well, it's reactive. You don't really think about what you're doing. Had I taken a moment to consider my actions, I wouldn't have created as big of a blast as I did. Instead of shocking the pixie, I pretty much discharged a lightning bolt inside the car.

The resulting shock wave burst the windows sending little chunks of safety glass outwards.

A horrendous blaring noise of six different alarms from several surrounding vehicles filled the air along with the smell of burnt upholstery. I fell back against the dashboard, briefcase in hand as both the pixies and the goblin had let go. One of the pixies flew forward and screamed at me, a high-pitched assault that I barely heard over the alarms.

I grabbed the door handle and quickly swung it open, hitting the vehicle parked in the next slot. About as gracefully as a drunken giraffe, I jumped out of the Cobalt and tried not to slip on the glass that now littered the ground. Briefcase clasped firmly to my chest, I skidded into a truck and ran forward away from the pixies... and towards the cops.

Both Harper and the uniform had their guns drawn at me, a sight I'm a little too familiar with these days. Thankfully they weren't trigger happy, just more confused than anything else. I can't imagine what the scene looked like to the policeman who, as far as I knew, was completely oblivious to the world of magic.

In situations like these, I like to take wisdom from Skipper: just smile and wave, Minni, smile and wave...

FOUR[4]

Well, I didn't get arrested this time, so I'm calling it a win.

I did have to sit in the back of a squad car for a bit while Harper smoothed things over. Harper convinced the other cops that Perkins's car must have been struck by lightning, or something. I was protected because I was in the 'cage' of the vehicle. Yeah, these guys weren't the sharpest sticks, you know?

I mean, I'm not sure how they could have missed that the bolt struck from the inside out, not the outside in. Let's just say they probably ain't going to make detective.

But now, thanks to me, the parking lot was an official 'crime scene,' which meant paperwork was involved and the place was swarming with cops. Okay, there was like six cops. Anyway, at least Perkins's briefcase was safely tucked away as evidence in one of the police cars, so the goblin and pixies couldn't get to it. Maybe. Hopefully.

We certainly couldn't get to it.

The pixie scratch on my arm was little more than red whelps. I blamed it on the car and was able to get a large square band-aid from the cops. At least I could keep the cut from getting infected before I had a chance to clean it proper. After that, they just left me to sit there in the cruiser while they did their thing.

I texted with Marcel while he was on a break, but he had to get back to work. Then, just as I got to my limit of how much of Twitter I could scroll through in one sitting, Harper finally came and sprung me.

"Did you give them my real name?" I asked quietly after I got out of the squad car. I kind of have a record with the police. I was "kidnapped" last year during the Delaware incident. Do not mock my finger quotes.

"I didn't give them any name. I told them you're Perkins's teaching assistant." He led me around the cruiser, a brown paper bag in his hand. "I said I would escort you to your car. I'm going to be taking care of most of the paperwork. I'll figure something out."

"Appreciate it." I was sincere because he really goes above and beyond for us wizards.

Harper nodded, then showed me the brown sack which turned out to be an evidence bag. "The OJ bottle was ignored as trash. Maybe Phil can do something with it?"

"Can't hurt."

We made our way out of the parking lot, putting distance between ourselves and the cops. "I'm going to pick up my car and follow the uniforms to their precinct. Hopefully I can get the briefcase out of lockup."

"Why did they take it anyway?" Seriously, it's not like an actual crime had been committed. That they knew of at least. Perkins was poisoned, but neither I, nor Harper, were inclined to share that information.

"Because I told them I was working a case," Harper explained. "If I just took it without following procedure then they would be suspicious. And they're kinda jerks."

Ugh. *Policemen.*

We stopped at a crosswalk and Harper asked, "Why did you set off a lightning bolt in the car, anyway?"

"I was being attacked by pixies and I wasn't sure whose side the goblin was on."

"Didn't you take on a dragon like, two months ago?"

"Yeah, but that was on purpose."

The cop let out a long sigh. "*Wizards.*"

Tell me about it.

We made it back to the shop without incident, the goblin and pixies having been sufficiently scared off. It seemed like they were only after the briefcase and couldn't get into a locked car. I don't know why they didn't break the window or something. It could have been a threshold issue.

We warned Harper to be careful with the briefcase anyway, and to make sure it stayed locked up. Phil also gave him the name of a Forsaken in the local precinct who could help. Harper left with this in mind, and I finally got to eat my sandwich. I was propped on a stool while Phil literally stared at the plastic bottle for a good ten minutes.

"Did you have to melt it?" he commented on the fact that one of the tendrils of my lightning bolt had struck close enough to the bottle to cause it to soften and collapse in on itself. I wonder how Harper snuck that by those cops? I'm pretty sure he had to use a knife to cut away part of the seat it was stuck to.

I hope Perkins has really good car insurance.

"It was a reactive strike," I explained as I finished re-washing and disinfecting the pixie bite. It didn't look that bad so I let it breathe and didn't bother to put another gauze patch on it. "There were pixies... and a goblin."

"Look anything like this?" Ryan had been sitting in 'his chair' in the corner with a book on his lap. He hopped up and brought it over for me to see.

"Pretty spot on actually," I said, noting the same facial shapes and knobby features as the one from the car.

"You found that fast." Phil looked suitably impressed.

"Went off a hunch." Ryan wasn't at all bashful. "That goblin is a kobold, and, well, kobold, cobalt..."

I stared blankly at him as the sheer weight of the coincident crushed a little bit of my soul. Perkins took that moment to groan, hack, tremble, then return to his regularly scheduled comatose state.

"Shouldn't we really take him to a hospital now?" I asked once I was sure the man was still asleep and hadn't died on us.

"The poison acted fast," Phil explained. "He didn't have a chance to truly deteriorate before his organs shut down. We fed him a herbal potion while you were out, basically a magical version of an IV drip. Right now he just needs rest while his body and the magic flushes the neutralized poison and fixes what needs to be fixed."

"You hear any more from Ricard?" I asked.

"He thinks he should be fine, but he gave me a few things to look out for. If Perkins starts to turn he'll hop through to the nearest Shadow Realm gate." Phil frowned. "I'd like to avoid that because Ricard charges triple for house calls."

"Alright." I wasn't about to argue with Phil, he knew what he was doing, usually. "Any word on the Cobalt Star yet?"

"No." His jaw twitched a bit. "And I've been looking."

"Why don't you google it?" Ryan asked.

Why do I keep forgetting I can do that?

I grabbed my phone and typed Cobalt Star into the search bar and let it do its thing.

"Somehow I don't think that's it." I frowned as I glanced through the first results. "Unless Perkins really loves *Mario Kart*."

"That's a video game, right?" Phil asked and it never ceases to amaze me what pop culture references he does and doesn't get.

"Yeah." I kept scrolling. "Apparently it's an item in one of the *Mario & Luigi* games."

"I'm gonna say that's probably not it then."

I gave a generally agreeable grunt. "Now, that is promising."

I found my personal space encroached upon as both Phil and Ryan decided they couldn't wait to see what I'd found. I clicked the Wikipedia link and the screen was filled with the image of a sapphire that had to be a bit bigger than a silver dollar. It was a rich blue color, struck through with a silver starburst pattern that was just slightly off center.

"Pretty." Ryan sounded like he wanted to steal it. Not that this would surprise anyone.

"The Cobalt Star," I read from the article, "also known as the Mostar Sapphire, is the third largest known star sapphire, weighing 527.26 carats. The cabochon-cut, cabinson? Cabocon?"

"Ka-ba-shon," Ryan pronounced correctly for me.

"The cabbage-cut gem," I'm from the Mid-West, I gave up caring years ago, "was discovered in the collection of Ivo Bugarski after he died at the end of World War II. Bugarski had made his fortune as a bauxite miner in Mostar, Bosnia-Herzegovina (then Yugoslavia). Bugarksi… blah blah blah…

"Okay, the Cobalt Star was sold at private auction by Christie's in 1947 to pay off Bugarski's debts. The gem currently remains in a private collection and has not come up for sale or auction since. It is still unknown when and where the gem was mined and cut."

"Bet you twenty bucks it's magical," Ryan said, then moved off toward one of the many piles of books in the room.

"Gem of that size?" Phil practically laughed. "If anything, it's got to have a high level of perception magic. Perhaps that's why Perkins is interested in the Cobalt Star?"

"Is he a Forsaken and I missed it?" Energy is my thing so I'm pretty good at picking out natural magic users when I'm actively looking for them. I didn't sense anything from Perkins but hey, I could have missed something.

"No," Phil assured me. "He is a teacher in environmental sciences. It's possible his interest is purely academic."

"Would someone really poison him over an academic interest?" I said and then held my hand up. "Never mind, I went to college. That's totally legit."

Ryan headed for the staircase. "Now that we know that it is, I'm going to pull all the magical gem books we have."

"Good idea." Phil went back to the table with the melted juice bottle. "I have a few more tricks up my sleeve. I might be able to get something from this."

As the other two wizards started to do their thing and be productive, I stole Phil's bag of chips. Hey, when it comes to magical research and the like, I am out of my depth. At least I recognize this.

About an hour passed and it was hedging past five. I got a text from Marcel. *"About to catch the train. What you want to do tonight?"*

"How about a quiet night in? My place." I replied to Marcel then grabbed Phil's attention. "So, Phil, I was thinking: if nothing really changes, I was going to head out in a bit."

Phil's brow pinched together as he fought off revealing a confused expression. "Not sure that's wise. There are kobolds and pixies out there."

"And vampires and lich and drunk drivers," I countered. "The way I see it, they weren't after me, they were after the briefcase, which is now locked up at the police station."

"They could follow you, thinking you'll lead them to it."

"And when they realize I haven't, they'll leave me alone, or I'll zap them again." I let out a very long sigh. "Look, Marcel and I have finally gotten back to a good place since the whole Canton thing. And the past two weekends have been hit and miss because I've been doing tour guide stuff. Now I actually have a holiday weekend to myself."

"And you want to spend it with him," Phil said softly. "I get it. I just don't want you to put yourself or him in danger."

"We'll stay at my place, protected by my wards. You know I won't let anything happen to Marcel."

"Sometimes, that's what I'm afraid of."

Phil's my friend—my magical BFF actually—but we didn't meet by chance. When I was in college, I, well… I murdered a man, back home in Nebraska. I don't regret it either. I saved my brother and for that you will never hear me apologize.

My punishment for manslaughter was to be quietly put away where I could still be useful, what with my talents regarding energy manipulation. Consider it a kind of probation, I guess. Phil was tasked with being my warden, yet another of the dozens of thankless, menial jobs thrown at him. I sometimes forget we were never supposed to be friends, but Phil doesn't.

"Found it." Ryan came bounding down the stairs, book in hand. He thumped a large tome on the table. "The Cobalt Star."

We moved over to see what he was pointing at. On the yellowed parchment was a drawing of a rounded off gem with a starburst pattern design. It matched the Wiki image near perfectly except that it was adorned on a different necklace. The one sold at Christies was a more modern, streamlined chain. The one drawn here was so ornate it looked like Roccoco threw up on Baroque.

"Is this German?" I frowned, not recognizing the words as English, Spanish, or Tsėhésenėstsestȯtse. Those are the only three languages I know. Ish.

"Norwegian, actually." Ryan frowned. If it was German, he could have read it.

"How do you know it's Norwegian?" Phil asked. As far as I know, he wasn't familiar with the language either. He's more of a Latin man.

"The preface is in like six different languages." Ryan gestured towards the front part of the book but didn't bother lifting the page. "Can you bring up that translation app again?"

I pulled out my phone and saw Marcel had already texted me back. He said it sounded good; he'd even cook. I sent back nothing but emojis because he is a damn fine cook and then switched over to the translation app. Once I made sure the phone was properly connected to my energy field and wouldn't short out, I gave it to Ryan. He proceeded to write stuff down on a piece of paper as he went.

"Kobolds," Ryan mumbled to himself. "The Cobalt Star is sacred to them."

"Because of course it is," I replied wryly.

"I'll need a few minutes," Ryan said as he grabbed a stool and settled in to the task.

Phil picked up the plastic bottle. "Well, at least I think I figured out our poison. Someone used magic to transfer thallium into the bottle from a distance."

"So he could have bought the OJ at a store along the way, or had it on him." I tried to follow the train of logic. "Either way, someone was watching him well enough to be able to set up and transfer the poison."

"That kind of transfer takes a few minutes to perform and complete." Phil glanced over at Perkins, then at me. "Whoever did it may still be watching him."

The point was taken about me leaving, but I ignored it. "I don't think it was the kobold or the pixies. They're more claws and teeth than cloak and dagger."

Phil gave a general nod of agreement. "Whoever it is, if they can pull off that kind of poisoning, then they're probably smart enough not to try to cross the shop wards. Perkins should be safe here."

"And I should be safe behind mine."

"Alright," Ryan spoke up, completely ignoring the uber-frown Phil was giving me. "I think I got this. Kobolds date back to at least the 13th Century. They're part of the House Spirits tradition, but they can be helpful or mischievous. The element cobalt was named after them because miners thought kobolds were responsible for the nasty nature of the element.

"Now, the Cobalt Star is a star-sapphire," Ryan continued. "Sapphires aren't mined in Eastern Europe. The Star literally randomly appears in Germany in the 1770s. There is no information whatsoever about who brought it in or where it was mined. It's suspected it came out of Sri Lanka, but that's just an educated guess."

"Can't they do like tests or something?" I asked. "Take a chip and determine all the little elements and carbons and stuff?"

"They did do tests in the 1940s." Ryan flipped the page. "Inconclusive. Maybe it was the tech at the time, maybe something more magical was going on."

"Maybe both," I said with a grimace. When tech and magic mix, things tend to get mucked up pretty royally.

"What happened in the 1770s?" Phil got us back on track.

Ryan turned to the previous page, pointing at text we couldn't read. "In 1772, the King of Denmark-Norway, wait, did I write that down right?"

"Denmark and Norway were united as a single entity for about three hundred years between the 1500s and 1800s," Phil said. Ryan and I both just looked at him without a single hint of surprise that he knew such a thing.

"Right." Ryan shook his head and continued. "The King of Denmark-Norway, one Christian the Seventh, presented the Cobalt Star to the workers of the Blaafarveværket. And I totally mis-pronounced that."

"The Blaafer-what?" You know what, I'm not even going to try. My sincerest apologies to the Norwegian language.

"It's this huge cobalt mine in Norway." Ryan moved the book so we could see a sketch of what I assume is typical classic Norwegian building techniques. Sloped roofs, white washed stone walls with crisscrossing beams. "Apparently it was pretty big business for Norway at the time."

"What happened?" Phil asked.

"The mine was shut in 1893." Ryan shrugged. "The official report is that cobalt became less economical to mine as cheaper alternatives were hitting the market."

"The unofficial report?"

"Well, the mine was doing well because of the Cobalt Star," Ryan explained, turning another page in the book to the sketch of a kobold. "The kobolds in the mine were helpful and didn't cause mischief which meant the miners could, well, mine the ore. Then in 1878, the Star disappeared, likely stolen, but the writer of this text couldn't find any details about it."

"The Cobalt Star goes away, and so does the kobolds' help." I catch on quick sometimes.

"Exactly." Ryan turned the page. "They might have stayed in business longer—even with the price of cobalt going down—if they didn't have angry kobolds to deal with."

"Why wasn't any of this on the Wiki article?" I asked. "It picks up in the 1940s."

"This section of the book was written in 1953," Ryan explained, the tome looking far older than that. It was probably because wizards still had to do things the old fashion way in the '50s. Typewriters are okay; they're mechanical. But even today, you'll see wizards hand-writing out all the important documents. "It was written in response to the Cobalt Star being found. The wizard's specialty was gem magic. It was only because she was from Norway that she knew of the connection to the mines. Apparently it was very difficult to find anything about the Star. There were no official records, everyone was long dead, and there were just bits and pieces to work off of."

"Did the author try talking to the kobolds?" Phil asked and I wondered if that was possible. Then I realized I was an idiot. What if the kobold was speaking Norwegian to me? I wish I'd paid more attention to the words and not the fact I didn't understand them.

"Only enough to know they were mad it was taken from them." Ryan closed the book. "She wrote the information down and it didn't really get shared with the non-magical community."

"I should totally edit that Wiki article," I said with a moderate amount of conviction.

"Whose sources are you gonna cite?" Phil asked with a raised brow.

"Point taken," I grumbled.

My phone went beep again and I picked it up from where Ryan had left it. The text was from Marcel saying he stopped to pick up groceries and gave me an ETA to my apartment. If I left then, I would just about beat him there.

I texted him back then addressed Phil. "Well, nothing we can do until either Perkins wakes up or Harper can get us his briefcase. I'll keep my phone and sender on me so you can contact me if anything changes and you need me to... dunno... power something or absorb something."

That's really all I'm good for.

"Be careful," Phil said with a very passive aggressive sigh.

"Aren't I always? ...Don't answer that."

FIVE[5]

A little past six am the next day I was woken up by Freddy Mercury. That's what happens when your ring tone for the Mercury Shop is set to Queen's *It's a Kind of Magic*.

I'd fallen asleep on the sofa sometime during the night. More actually, I had fallen asleep against Marcel who was sitting on the sofa. He was tucked into the corner and I was spread out across the cushions using his torso as a pillow. As it should be.

To be fair, it was probably less comfortable for him than it was for me. Which, now that I think about it, is a perfect metaphor for our relationship.

I grabbed my phone and sat up, letting the groggy nausea pass as my brain seemed to have woken up before my body did. Marcel shifted a bit but otherwise did not wake.

"What?" I said into the phone once I managed to answer.

"Harper is bringing the briefcase." Phil is never fazed by my lack of decorum early in the mornings. "Perkins is going to wake up soon. Can you come down to the shop?"

I glanced over at Marcel, who snoozed peacefully. It was Saturday, there was so much we could do, some of it even involving leaving the apartment.

"Give me a few to shower," I told Phil with a sigh. I could just walk away. I did my part and helped, after all. But if this was connected to what happened with Delaware, Canton, and the dragons, then it was probably best I kept on it.

"Alright," there was a little relief in his voice. "Just be careful. We don't know if the kobolds or pixie's are still out there or after you."

"Yeah, I know." I stretched, my body tensing while every bone seemed to pop. "I'll see you in a bit."

I took a quick shower and by the time I was finished, Marcel was awake. I told him I had to go to Phil's shop and help out but that I'd see him later that day. He wasn't terribly happy about it, but he didn't argue the point with me either. He knows that Phil and the coven are important to me, even if he doesn't know that we're actually a coven of magic users.

I don't know why he puts up with me.

Hell, I don't know why I put up with me.

Anyway, I stopped by Dunkin' Donuts on my way, of course, to grab coffees for everyone and a fifty pack of Munchkins.

"Did I miss any excitement?" I asked as Ryan let me in through the front door of the shop.

"Not really," he said as he took the coffee carrier from me. "Someone, or something, did have a go at the wards at about two this morning."

I snorted. "How did that go for them?"

Ryan chuckled. We both know just how strong Phil's wards are on the shop. Sure, as a public location the threshold is a bit weak, but once the store is closed the place locks down tighter than Fort Knox against anything magical. And that's before Phil strengthened them because of the high likelihood of such an attack.

"How about you?" Ryan asked as we crossed into the back room where Perkins had been left to recover on the sofa.

"Not a peep," I told him as I sat the Munchkins on the table next to Perkins' briefcase. "I strengthened my wards just in case, but not so much a gnat tried to get in."

"That's good to hear," Phil said as he walked in, Harper in tow. "It was a bit of a risk for you to leave."

I'd heard plenty of that from him last night. "The kobolds and pixies are after Perkins and/or the Cobalt Star. They're not going to come all the way to New York from Norway to just wing it... Pun not intended." Okay, a little intended.

"So you believe." Phil grabbed his coffee from the drink carrier.

See, Phil, I love him to death; he's like a fifth brother to me. But, if I'm being honest, I'm often unsure he actually cares about my health and wellbeing, or if he's really good at pretending that he does to keep me in line. And this is why you should never make friends with your jailers.

"Alright." I put it all behind me because it's what I do. "What's the plan?"

"Ryan has figured out the combination." Phil pointed at the briefcase. "I want you to open it."

"Okay," I said as I rolled up the sleeves of shirt. My actual shirt this time. I didn't steal anything from Marcel because when magic is involved there is always the likelihood of clothing getting ripped or burnt or something really gross spilt on it, like dragon bile. You know, I thought I was over that. Guess not. "What kind of magic am I dealing with?"

"I don't sense any magic," Phil admitted. "Either there are no wards on the briefcase, or something really subtle and nasty is happening here."

"Oh, great," I said with a complete lack of enthusiasm.

Taking a deep breath, I planted my feet firmly in front of the briefcase should there be a physical component to the wards. Sometimes just a blast of magical energy can be solid enough to knock you off your feet. I then placed both hands on the two release catches so I could open them at the same time.

One more deep breath and I hit the buttons, ready to drain away whatever spell came at me.

Nothing happened except for the sharp clack of the locks flipping up. So far, so good. But I kept myself on guard as I slowly raised the lid. I sent out tendrils of energy and received no pushback.

"It's clean," I said when I was 99.98% sure.

I was kind of expecting something spectacular when I looked inside, like maybe the infamous Cobalt Star. Instead, it was full of what you'd expect from a teacher. There was just a bunch of files, pens, a pack of gum, those kinds of things.

"Well, that's disappointing." Ryan, good at obvious.

"Let's see what we have," Phil said as he proceeded to pull out the files. I backed off and let the professionals deal with it.

I grabbed my coffee and went over to check on Perkins. He did look a lot better than last I saw him. The color was back in his skin and he didn't look as clammy or ill. He did smell a bit, but you know, I wasn't going to blame him on that one. Not his fault someone poisoned him into a stupor… Probably.

"This looks interesting," Harper said as he passed a piece of paper over to Phil.

"Is that what I think it is?" Ryan asked as he stuffed a Munchkin in his mouth.

"If you think it's a retrieval spell, yeah." Phil's brow pinched and he headed over to the bookcase, and grabbed one of his many tomes. "It's for the Cobalt Star."

"A retrieval spell? Is it what it sounds like?" Harper asked.

"Probably," Phil muttered and went nose deep into the book. He wasn't coming out of it for a few minutes.

"It's basically a dual locator spell and matter transfer spell," I explained as I sipped my coffee.

Harper frowned, crossing his arms. "You know, sometimes when you all speak, I'm not sure if I'm in an episode of *Supernatural* or *Star Trek*."

"Dude." Ryan grinned. "You're in the *Matrix*, duh."

I gave the kid an approving smirk.

"My apologies," Harper replied dryly.

I think locator spells are cool because there are so many types of them. Most usually involve having a piece to locate the whole, but as you know there's always a workaround. As for a matter transfer spell, those are a lot trickier. You take an object and literally move it—usually through the Shadow Realm—to your location. Sometimes you even have to bend space or break down an item to its molecular level.

So, yeah, okay, that's totally a transporter from *Star Trek*.

Anyway, if you put the two spells together you can target a specific item, wherever it might be, and make it come to you. It's magic that should only be left to seasoned magic users.

"You think that's why he came here?" I stared down at Perkins. "He isn't a magic user, but needed one to enact the spell?"

"Isn't there a coven outside Wilmington?" Ryan asked.

"There is," Phil answered as he put his book down. "It's possible he didn't know about them. I've pretty well established the Mercury Shop as a haven for magic users on the upper East Coast."

"Didn't take me long to find it." Ryan nodded. He'd been living upstairs for a few years now. He ran away from home once he was legally able to do so. Can't rightly blame him though, all things considered. I'm just glad it worked out in his favor, as it so often doesn't.

"There is another possibility." Phil frowned, slightly narrowing his eyes at Perkins. "I also have one of the largest collections of rare books on the East Coast. He could have simply wanted to read that." He pointed at the gem book Ryan had pulled from upstairs. "He may not know magic is real."

"He's Welsh," I pointed out.

"That's generalizing." Phil gave me a slightly disapproving look. "Just because he's Welsh doesn't mean he believes in magic."

Alright, he had me there.

"Are we going to try the spell?" Harper asked the room.

Phil rubbed his chin. He does that a lot. Probably why he can't grow a beard. "We'll wait till Perkins wakes up. Should be soon."

"He does look better than last I saw," I commented as I went back to my perch on the stool.

As if he heard us talking about him, Perkins started to shift a bit, coughing to clear out his throat. Ryan was closer to him, so he went to the man's side to see if he needed any help.

I heard Phil lean over to Harper and whisper, "We assume he's a non-believer until otherwise confirmed."

Harper nodded and joined Ryan who was crouched next to the sofa. "Mr. Perkins, you're safe."

That did little to calm the agitated man who opened his glassed over eyes, blinked several times, and started to cough.

Ryan grabbed a bottle of water from the side table. "Here, drink." He held the bottle to Perkins's lips. The man spilled more than he gulped, but it seemed to help. His breathing started to slow down and his eyes refocused. His lids fluttered closed and I am pretty sure he fell asleep for a straight five minutes before stirring again. I think his body just had to do a reboot.

Perkins looked at us with tired and confused eyes. He then grabbed his stomach and made that wet gurgle sound that is often the precursor to hurling. Thankfully there was a trashcan within reach. Phil grabbed it and quickly put it next to Perkins as he rolled over to puke blue. Ryan tried to backpedal but only ended up on his rear. Harper grabbed Perkins to keep him steady.

I completely lost my appetite and put my coffee down. I even stopped reaching for the remaining Munchkins. I swear those things just disappear around me.

"Where? What?" I'm pretty sure that's what Perkins said.

"You're at the Mercury Shop, Brooklyn," Phil explained. "I'm the owner, Phillip McCree."

"Mercury Shop?" Perkins echoed as he seemingly bounced the name around his head.

"You stumbled into my shop," Phil added. "It could have been a mistake?"

Perkins did seem hella confused but that was probably from the fact he just woke up from almost dying.

"Mr. Perkins, I'm Detective Harper, NYPD. Did you know you were poisoned?"

Way to be direct there, Harper.

"Poisoned?" Perkins shook his head. "I was... I was..."

"Take your time," Harper said gently. "You're safe now."

"*Seren cobalt.*" Perkins started to look around frantically, nearly clawing at Phil and Harper. "*Seren cobalt.*"

"*Seren cobalt,*" Phil repeated gently, mangling the words a little less than I did. "We know about the Cobalt Star. Are you looking for it?"

"I..." Perkins's breathing was jagged and his eyes were still a little glazed over. "I have to find it before it's too late."

And then he passed out again leaving us to stare at each other like there *wasn't* an ominous threat now hanging over our heads.

You know, I was starting to like the guy.

SIX[6]

Perkins passed out for only a couple of minutes. When he woke up again he asked for the bathroom. All things considered, it was in our best interests to let the man spend a few minutes freshening up.

There's a toilet on the bottom floor, for customers only and all that. Perkins disappeared into it while Ryan went upstairs to grab something for Perkins to wear. Since the Mercury Shop is a stop off point for wizards, Phil had a room that looked like a survivalist's wet dream. There was personal hygiene stuff, spell components, and an assortment of basic t-shirts and sweatpants in various sizes.

Phil didn't kid around when it came to being a safe place for wizards to come to when they got stuck in New York City. Sometimes it was lost wizards, other times it was wizards who had been traveling awhile and just needed a place to stop and rest. Phil's door was open to anyone who needed help.

Probably why he got saddled with me.

Ryan came back with a pile of clothes, a small travel toothbrush kit, and wet wipes. He knocked on the door and told Perkins he had supplies for him. The door opened a moment later and Perkins gratefully took the stuff. He glanced at us awkwardly though, not that I blamed him. All four of us were just standing there, staring at him because, well, Phil and Harper wanted answers, Ryan was right in front of him, and I... was still there.

Several minutes later, Perkins finally shuffled out of the bathroom. He looked refreshed, or the closest he could get, considering the circumstances.

"Uh." Perkins cleared his throat which still ended up sounding raspy. "I was poisoned?"

"You weren't aware of this?" Harper asked as he gestured for Perkins to sit down.

"I just started to feel... ill," Perkins replied with a hopeless shrug and sunk down into the offered chair. He had an accent, which sounded kind of familiar, but not quite British. Not that I'm an expert on the subject.

Ryan came up beside him and held out a bottle of water and food. "Protein bar," he told Perkins. "It's that or a peanut butter sandwich but I didn't know if you had an allergy."

"No allergies, thank you." Perkins took the items with a pitiful smile. The man looked like he had no strength in his body, the epitome of running on fumes.

Harper gave Perkins a moment to drown some water before asking, "What was your destination when you left Dover?"

"The Mercury Shop, Brooklyn." He got a little hazy, then his eyes widened as if he remembered something. "My briefcase. I had important documents in my briefcase."

"We got it right here." Harper put a gentle hand on the man's shoulder and gestured over to the table. "And you're at the Mercury Shop. This is the owner, Phillip McCree."

"Hi," Phil managed to say in a way that wasn't awkward. "Were you coming to see me?"

"Yes." Perkins nodded and then zoned out again. I was about to ask if maybe we should let him take another nap but he came to. "I need to locate the Cobalt Star."

"The sapphire?" Phil asked for clarification. After Perkins nodded, Phil continued with, "It was sold at Christie's in the '40s."

"Yes, and they don't give out customer information. Bad for business and all that." Perkins said before finishing off the bottle of water. "What I could find said that it was bought through an agent who passed away years ago."

Not bad, Perkins. You did your research.

Phil gave his little pensive face. "How did you think I could help?"

"I..." Perkins started to breathe a little heavier, his body slumping slightly. "I made a deal with a fae."

Perkins, you are an effing idiot.

"Okay," Phil said calmly, amazingly unjudgmental even though I could see him almost try to cross his arms. "What was the name of the fae?"

"Avalbane of the Seelie Court."

Well, at least that was something.

The fae come from their own section of the Shadow Realm, but unlike other shadow creatures, fae aren't made from shadow stuff. They're made from magic itself. Since magic is energy and cannot be created nor destroyed, fae are about as unkillable as it gets. They also have no ichor or blood that you can use to perform spells on them with. They are resistant to most all magic. Also, they're smug little bastards, even more so than dragons.

The Seelie Court is the 'light' side to the 'dark' side that is the Unseelie Court. But there isn't a heck of a lot of difference between the two. It's like choosing between the Irish and Sicilian mobs. You know, I probably shouldn't be comparing fae to mobsters, but then my ability not to antagonize people who could easily kill me has always been a little iffy.

"Avalbane," Phil repeated. He gestured towards Ryan, who quickly made his way upstairs. Turning back to Perkins, Phil asked, "What were the terms of the deal?"

"I was to locate the Cobalt Star," he replied weakly. "In return, Avalbane would ensure I would never be found wanting."

"That's old school," I mused out loud.

Harper scrunched his brow like he didn't care if people saw he had no clue what was going on. "What does piousness have to do with anything?"

"Cross cultural idioms," Phil explained as Ryan came back into the room, yet another book in hand. I swear they just appear out of thin air in that place. "When a fae says never to be found wanting, it means they will ensure you have a long life with good health and comfortable living."

"Okay, sounds enticing." Harper bobbed his head lightly. "What's the catch?"

Phil took the book and laid it on the table. "With the fae,

one can never be too sure. They're hard pressed not to find loopholes in carefully worded statements."

"They don't want keep their end of the deal?"

"No, they're happy to, mostly because they are bound by ancient laws, but they're also immortals who bore easily." Phil shrugged. "If you leave them an opening to entertain themselves, they'll take it."

"Exactly," Perkins agreed. "But Avalbane came to me. I did not seek her out."

Phil's head popped up. "She came to you?"

"It was about two weeks after that solar flare thing." Perkins cleared his throat. "At least that is what the news was calling it. I'm sure it was magical."

We all exchanged looks at this point. Totally not subtle. But you know, so what if we misplaced Delaware for a few minutes? Completely the dragon's fault.

"Did Avalbane say anything else?" Phil was now more interested in Perkins than the book.

"Nothing." He shook his head lightly. "She was pretty straight forward. Find the Cobalt Star, give her said Cobalt Star, and I would never be found wanting."

"There was no caveat?" Phil asked, confused. "No 'if you don't do this within three moons you'll be stricken ill'?"

"I made sure to ask if there was punishment for failing the task," Perkins said emphatically. "I know how the fae can be. But she left it open, no deadline."

Phil scratched between his brows as he thought about the situation. I couldn't understand it either. It was unusual for a fae to leave things open ended. That was usually part of the fun. They promise you riches but only if you can master underwater basket weaving in four hours.

"While you were coming to," Harper started, "you said you had to find the Cobalt Star before it was too late."

Nice catch there, but Perkins just looked more confused. "I don't remember saying that. I suppose part of me was worried if I took too long, Avalbane will rescind her offer."

Made sense. But where is the game in all of this?

"Avalbane is a low level fae," Phil eventually said, going back to the book. "She has the ability to give you a comfortable life, but not even trying to make it a challenge isn't going to win her any points if she's looking to up her standing."

"Maybe that's why she's still low level?" I mused. "She's too nice for her own good?"

Harper let out a thoughtful sigh. "Someone nearly killed him over this chunk of jewelry. Maybe that's the challenge?"

"Man has a point," Ryan helpfully agreed.

Phil wasn't totally convinced. "Why did Avalbane come to you? Were you already connected to the Cobalt Star?"

"After a fashion." Perkins rubbed his forehead and looked like he might pass out again. "I teach environmental sciences and I've done work in geochemistry. I am by no means a global expert, but I know a fair bit about gemstones."

"Did you ever study the Cobalt Star directly?" Phil asked.

"No, it never came up."

"Can you think of any reason why Avalbane would come to you?" Phil tried again.

"I'm sorry." Perkins continued to shake his head. "I can't."

"Maybe it's because he drives a blue Cobalt?" I ventured, which garnered me questionable looks from everyone in the room. "Hey, fae tend to get confused. They have no concept of the human perception of time, or even the eccentricities of human emotions. It's the only way you can beat them, usually."

"She wasn't confused," Perkins assured me. "She called me by name. My full name."

"Damn," the three wizards all said at once.

"You have to have a connection to the Star." Phil rubbed at his chin, again. "Your bio says you're a Welsh immigrant. Did your family ever have dealings with the Twith Twyg?"

Those are the fairies native to Wales by the way.

"I wouldn't know." Perkins frowned which made him look even more gaunt and sickly. "I didn't even know magic existed until after the flare incident, or whatever it was."

"How *did* you learn about magic?" Phil asked.

"Whatever caused the disruption led to a shadow demon escaping unchecked into our world. It didn't do any real damage, but it did terrorize the campus. A group of wizards took care of it and I kind of fell into the middle of the situation."

"Who was the coven leader?" Phil asked.

"Francis, Francis Cuellar."

"I know him," Phil responded, moving to grab his sender from the countertop. "Did he send you to me?"

"No, he honestly didn't want any part of this." Perkins slumped down into his chair. "But I remembered something he had said before. That if we couldn't stop the demon that got loose then he'd call Phillip McCree of the Mercury Shop, Brooklyn. If anyone could stop it, he could."

See, Phil, this is what happens when you build a reputation. You actually have to deliver on said reputation. By the look on Phil's face, he wasn't keenly comfortable with the idea.

"What about the transporter spell you brought?" Harper asked, gesturing toward the parchment sitting on the table. "Did you write that yourself?"

"Oh, dearie, no." Perkins's Welsh accent got a little thicker and he almost laughed. "I found it. I asked Francis to cast it for me, but he said no, that it was too dangerous."

"Where did you find it?" I asked.

"I went back to the last known owner, Ivo Bugarski," he explained. "His entire estate was sold off. That included his home, his business, personal effects. It took some doing, and some help, but I discovered a stash of paperwork that had been shoved in the back of a file room of the current mining company headquarters. The spell was in it. I think it's how Ivo got the Star himself."

"And when was this?" Harper asked.

"I spent two weeks in Mostar, Herzegovina. I got back on Sunday and talked to Francis on Tuesday."

"It's Saturday by the way," I pointed out. "You lost a whole day." I like being helpful.

Perkins looked absolutely stricken.

With a bit of a hum, Phil picked up the transfer spell and scanned over it again. "The spell does require a lot of components, but nothing I don't have on hand."

"You want to cast it?" Harper asked.

"Why not?" Phil took the yellowed paper over to the bookcase and started to treat it like a shopping list. "Someone was willing to murder over the Cobalt Star. The best way to make sure they don't hurt anyone else is to get the Star, figure out why it's worth killing over, and put it in the proper hands."

I cleared my throat. "You do realize that would make us targets, right?"

Phil gestured between himself, Harper, and I. "I think between the three of us we can handle it."

"Hey!" Ryan yelped indignantly.

"Francis said the spell was dangerous," Perkins reminded us. "I was mostly coming for a second opinion, or other options."

"Francis was right," Phil said as he piled stuff into the crook of his arm. "The spell is dangerous, but only for low-level wizards. Someone with his skill shouldn't really have a problem with it, unless maybe he's not particularly comfortable with these kinds of spells."

"He didn't elaborate."

"Just give me a few minutes." Phil placed the items on the table then started walking to the front. "With any luck, maybe we can all get out of here by lunchtime."

I figured that probably meant I'd be stuck there till dinner. So while Phil did his thing, I propped my feet up and started texting Marcel. Just the usual nothingness that felt like something because it came from him. He made me chuckle a few times which gained the occasional raised brow from whoever happened to be in hearing distance.

Man, I really miss him right now. I can't wait for this to all be over. I hate having to lie to him, again. Of course, I could just tell him the truth.

Yeah, no, that's not going to happen.

What can I say? I'm paranoid and selfish. Never denied it.

Over an hour later, Phil had everything sorted out on the table. He'd drawn a pictogram on the oak surface in chalk paste. Throughout it he placed six crystals made of conundrums, no, wait, corundums? Sorry, I was only half listening to him as he worked.

"I think we're ready to do this," Phil said, taking one last look at the spell.

I put my phone on silent and tucked it into my back pocket. I gestured for Harper to do the same. Harper probably didn't have a signal in there, but it's better to be safe than sorry. We didn't want the ringers to go off while Phil was trying to concentrate. Perkins's phone was still dead. I probably should have charged it for him. It really didn't matter now. Ryan had taken him upstairs to let him borrow the shower.

Phil stood before the table and took a deep breath, letting it out slowly. He spread his hands the width of the pictogram and began to recite the words of the spell. It was in Latin, which had led to an interesting argument regarding the origin of the Cobalt Star since Norwegian is a Germanic language. I'm not sure what one has to do with the other. You can write a spell in any language. I've seen them in Elvish *and* Klingon, true fact.

The wind started to pick up inside the room due to the temperature inversion caused by the spell drawing in energy. I could feel it, tugging at everything metaphysical. A pressure built around my chest, like I was standing in a closed water tank. Not enough to make it hard to breath, but the spell made itself known.

Phil's shoulders slumped and he started to lower his arms. "That's not right."

Yeah, not what you want to hear from a high level wizard when they're casting a spell.

"What's wrong?" Harper asked, nearly stepping forward but having the sense not to get too close.

The wind blew faster as a blue swirl of light built up above the table. The tightness in my chest grew and I started to siphon the energy away. But it was stretchy like a rubber band, pinching against my grasp.

"Shit, shit, shit!" Phil waved his arms in a pattern, trying to control whatever forces he had called forward. The spell only intensified. "MINNI!"

Phil shouted and I reacted. I rushed forward and pushed him to the side. As he lost connection, the magic whiplashed. It would have exploded against itself but I caught it instinctively. The magic burned against my metaphysical grip as I held on tight.

"You got it?!" Phil yelled against the howling wind.

"Yeah," I managed through gritted teeth.

The more I tried to siphon the energy into my aura, the more it pinched. If I kept going, the stream wouldn't just break off, it would snap. I needed to get the magic to go back where it came from, preferably without it whipping around like a broken power line.

I closed my eyes and reopened them using my Third Eye. With it, I could see the energy I held, not just the sparkly after effects of the corona. The stream was coming from a portal that had formed over the pictogram. It swirled violently, like Charydbis when he's feeling particularly hungry.

Slowly, I fed the energy back to itself, releasing the tension bit by bit. Just when I thought maybe I had this under control, the spell rotated on its event horizon. My feet literally scooted on the concrete floor as it tugged violently, wanting to collapse.

"Who fucking designed this thing!?" I screamed, planting my feet as best I could.

"Minni!" I heard Phil yell again. I could barely see him moving around in my peripherals.

I don't know what he thought he was going to do. Energy is my thing, but this spell was literally designed to explode. That's when I realized that the only way out was through, I was probably the only witch designed to be able to take the brunt of it.

"This is gonna suck," I said before making yet another in a long line of questionable decisions.

I stopped fighting it, letting the stream pull back. But I held on and kept it steady, let it collapse in on itself neatly instead of violently. This meant allowing it to use me as a stabilizing agent. I reached out and helped hold the ends, bringing them together as the portal shut down… with me on the other side.

I was jerked off my feet and flew into the table. I barely registered hitting it with my leg as the portal sucked me in. My body became enveloped in that same feeling of pressure, of being submerged in water with my head just barely above the surface. I tumbled ass over tea kettle in a bright blue light, chasing shadows at the edge of my vision.

Just as I had a second to breathe, I was thrown out the other end. All I saw was my reflection as I hit the solid surface of water. It broke apart to swallow me into its depths.

The force of the impact caused me to inhale a deep breath, but all I got was water. My lungs burned and I lost all thought save a desire to breathe. My eyes were open but I couldn't focus. My arms and legs flailed but I had no control, no idea which way was up.

Not for the first time in my life, I was pretty sure I was going to die. It was cold and solid realization. My mind was empty, not a single blessing or regret.

Two hands grabbed at me and pulled me to the surface. I coughed and wanted to vomit. As I bounced in the water, unable to get myself under control, I nearly choked on air as I was dragged to the edge of what I later discovered was a pool. Many hands hauled me onto the tiled poolside and then I threw up.

I spat out chlorine through my mouth and nose. My rescuer held me steady, pressing one hand on my spine to keep my chest open as I rapidly took in oxygen. When it seemed like I wasn't actively dying anymore, I collapsed onto my side.

I felt like shit, but I was alive.

"We really need to stop meeting like this."

I turned my head to see Aiden-the-fucking-asshole-Drake crouched over me with his dumb frosted tips dripping water onto my face.

Ugh, *dragons*.

SEVEN[7]

"Drake?" I didn't really mean it to be a question, but it came out that way.

"Miss Masterson." He sat back, his hand on my hip as if he was afraid I might roll over and die. To be fair, I was considering it. "Why don't we get you up off the floor first, then we can start the third degree."

I hate it when he's right.

Drake, sorry, *Mr. Aiden Drake, CEO of Pennington-Kettering Enterprises*, is a European gold dragon. He used a spell to take on a human form. I guess you can say he's an acquaintance of sorts?

Long story short, I saved his father during the whole Delaware/Canton incident. Canton was going to use Drake's father, Ignatius Drake, as a power source to destroy the world. Or maybe just Manhattan, still haven't figured that out yet.

As for Drake himself, I owed him a slap across the face because the whole time he kept messing with my friend, Stacey, casting suggestion spells on her. Luckily for him, I was in no shape to do much than lay there wearing wet sneakers, trying to remember how to breath.

Pulling me to my feet, Drake sat me down in a patio chair. I was in some kind of indoor swimming area. One wall of the enclosure was all windows, a nice stretch of countryside beyond. I knew I wasn't in Brooklyn anymore, but it really didn't click, you know?

The pool itself wasn't huge, not like Olympic size or anything. I don't know if it was a coincidence I hit it and not the solid ground. Not sure if I would have survived such a forceful impact against tile and stone—not that I had much chance surviving the water without someone to pull me out.

Drake was dressed in slacks and a Henley shirt which were now soaked through with water. There was no doubt he was the one who dived in to rescue me. With his golden tanned skin and hair the color of burnished gold, he almost looked god-like with the sun setting behind him through the windows. Not that I would tell him that; his ego doesn't need any help.

And Marcel wears a Henley way better anyway.

"Sir." Drake's butler made me nearly jump out of my skin as he stood next to us. His pants and jacket sleeves also wet. He was the second pair of hands hauling me out of the pool. "I have spoken to the doctor. He will be here in fifteen minutes."

"I'm fine." I still tasted chlorine.

"You almost drowned," Drake said emphatically in his odd English accent, which was not at all like what I'm used to hearing on television. "There could be complications and I'm not really up to explaining a dead American in my natatorium today."

"Nata-what?"

"As much as I am delighted by your company," Drake was totally not delighted, "would you please explain why you fell out of a portal and into my swimming pool?"

"I was trying to keep a spell from collaps—Phil!" I reached for my phone only to find it missing out of my back pocket.

Both of us looked to the pool.

Drake asked, "I don't suppose it's waterproof?"

"Ah, damnit." I sunk a little farther into the chair.

"This is starting to become a very bad habit." Drake grinned and I swear if I wasn't so exhausted I would have slapped him right then. Wouldn't have been the first time.

He was of course referring to the first time we met. I kind of accidently absorbed some of his draconic fire breathing magic. I couldn't control it and things got a little out of hand. I ended up at the bottom of a bathtub after having set Phil's bathroom on fire.

Yeah, that weekend… Not one of my best.

Drake gestured to his butler who handed him a phone. Unlocking it, he passed it to me. "Here, call Mr. McCree. Let him know you survived your ordeal."

I took it warily. "You're being awfully nice, Drake."

"I'm distracted," he replied tersely. "I would like to have this dealt with and you on your way as soon as possible."

I always feel more comfortable around Drake when he's making veiled threats.

Thankfully there was a search bar app at the top of the front screen because I don't have the shop number memorized. I did take a moment to note that Drake's wallpaper was that of vein of gold ore. I typed in Mercury Shop, Brooklyn, New York, and it came back with the business information. I clicked dial and hoped the shop phone hadn't shorted out.

After three rings, someone picked up. "Yeah, what?"

"Ryan?" I recognized his voice. "It's me, Minni."

"Minni!" Ryan nearly shouted, then he yelled into the distance. "She's not dead!"

As there was a shuffle with the phone, it suddenly clicked with me that the sun was slowly starting to set when it wasn't even lunch time moments before.

Hey, I almost drowned, I'm allowed to be a little slow.

Anyway, I pulled the phone away from my ear and looked at the clock. It was nearly four p.m. "Holy Hannah! Did I just lose five hours?"

"After a fashion." Drake was looking over his shoulder at the sunset. "You're at my estate north of Swansea, Wales."

"Wales? As in England?"

"As in Wales."

"Oh… great…"

"Minni," Phil's voice came over the line. "Where are you? Are you okay? I can come get you."

"I almost drowned, but I'm okay, except wet jeans are a horrible thing." They really are, not to mention wet socks in sneakers. And my leg was sore from hitting the table. It would be bruised for days. If I wasn't so happy to be alive, I'd been miserable. "As for where, I got thrown out in Wales, but specifically at our friend Drake's house."

There was a short pause. "Aiden?"

"Yep."

"That… Did you ask him about the Cobalt Star?"

"I haven't even dried off yet," I groused and like freaking magic, the butler appeared with two towels in hand. "You want me to ask him?"

There was another pause, this one long enough to allow me to quickly run a towel over my head and face, then wrap it around my neck. Eventually Phil said, "The spell was sabotaged, Minni. I see it now; it was very well hidden. Drake was also involved in the Delaware incident. Hell, he caused it. If this sent you to him, then I want to know why."

"Alright," I sighed and noticed that a gentleman was being shown into the pool house, a medical bag in hand. "The doctor's here, I gotta go."

"Doctor?" Phil asked.

"Yeah, almost drowned, I mentioned that, right?" I didn't give him time to voice a comeback. "I'll be in touch after I know more."

Hanging up with Phil, the phone did the most interesting thing. It popped up the dialing history of the number for the Mercury Shop. It looked like Drake had dialed it a dozen-ish times in the last two months. I wanted to ask him about it, but the doctor started to examine me and I got distracted. Then all this happened, and well, I'll eventually get around to asking him because that was weird.

The doctor was a legit doctor, not a magic user, not even a Forsaken. He sat me up straight, checked my lungs, my breathing, my oxygen levels, and whatever else. This meant him putting a very cold stethoscope against my already semi-freezing skin. Good times.

"What do you know about the Cobalt Star?" I asked Drake. I'm not very good with subtlety.

Drake gave me a very disappointed look. "Is that what this is about? Honestly, I would have thought you and Phil above such things."

Yeah, so, I was really confused. "Above what things?"

"The power of the Cobalt Star is just a myth," he dismissed me. "It's only good for making nice with kobolds, and I would hardly call that cosmic changing."

"Kay, you lost me."

Drake narrowed his eyes. "You *were* trying to find the Cobalt Star using a retrieval spell you found, correct?"

"Yes..."

"The spell failed because it was sabotaged," he continued to rattle off. "You managed survived the portal because of your... uniqueness."

"Why do I feel like you know more about what happened than I do, and I lived it?"

"Does she check out alright, doctor?" Drake asked him.

"Lungs sound clear and her oxygen levels are good," he replied in what I think of as a very typical British accent. "She should be watched for the next twenty-four hours. If she shows any respiratory distress or further vomiting, take her immediately to the hospital. She should avoid air and shadow travel for the next twenty-four hours as high pressure changes could cause fluid to build in her lungs."

"Twenty-four hours?" I couldn't even completely process what that meant for me. "This sucks..."

"Thank you, doctor." Drake dismissed him then turned to me. "Come, I'll explain."

"Right, but first." I kicked my sneakers off and proceeded to pull at my soaked socks. "Sorry, that was bugging the hell out of me."

Drake looked to the butler. "Prepare one of the guest rooms. Have a selection of Nev's wardrobe brought up. They were about the same size."

"Nev?" I asked as I stood, tossing away the now wet towel in favor of the dry one.

"This way." Drake didn't answer and instead started walking off. Whiffs of mist trailed from his body. It was water vapor: he was using thermal heat to dry himself. It's a neat trick and I could have done it myself, but I try to avoid casting too many spells right after almost dying. That's usually a good way to put myself in the hospital. I speak from experience.

We walked out of the pool house which was connected to the main house by a short, encased walkway. I couldn't tell you the age of the house or its style, only that it looked like the set of some period drama. No open concept here. Long hallways, ornate moldings, and décor straight out of a Jane Austin novel were the order of the day.

"Are you having a party?" I asked after we passed what looked to be a dining hall. Two waiters were in the middle of setting a long table where dozens of wine glasses waited to be filled.

"I am having dinner guests tonight, yes." He did not sound very happy about it. But I got the feeling he was less happy with the fact that I crashed said party.

Drake led us into a room that I guess was the parlor, but I'm not really sure. I know all these rooms have fancy names. But it wasn't a library, it wasn't a billiards room, and I think studies are supposed to have desks in them. This one just had a bunch of chairs, a nice big window, and a display case across one wall. There were a great many beautiful things in it, most of them gold.

Sitting on a headless, porcelain bust laid a ruby necklace, diamonds surrounding the quarter sized cabbage-cut stone. The deep red of the ruby was struck through with a six-line starburst pattern, just like the Cobalt Star.

"It is called the Star of Serendipity," Drake explained, opening the case. "It was mined in Sri Lanka, a very long time ago, when the island was called Serendip by the Persians. This is, of course, the root of where we get the word serendipity."

Okay, déjà vu. "What is your obsession with etymology?"

Drake gently lifted the necklace from the bust. "If you can't appreciate the intricacies of language and how it changes over time, then I'm afraid we can't be friends."

"I'm okay with that." I'm pretty sure we were never friends. "I'm still pissed at you about Stacey. I haven't punched you yet only because you did just save my life."

He didn't look terribly hurt by my admission. Instead he held up the necklace in two hands, giving the universal gesture of 'turn around so I can put this on you.'

I raised my brow. "Are you kidding me?"

"I am trying to prove a point." He repeated the gesture.

I decided I was too tired to care and it wasn't worth the argument. I turned around, one hand pulling away the towel while the other grabbed the damp mass of my hair, getting it out of the way. He placed the Star of Serendipity around my neck and quickly did the clasp. The chain was made of interwoven pieces of silver which were cold against my skin. It made me nervous to have such an expensive piece of jewelry on my person.

"It's not magical," I commented as I turned back. The only energy I could feel was some perception magic from the fact that it was a valuable item. Anyone can feel that kind of magic.

"Exactly." Drake seemed pleased that he had proven his point, except I wasn't a hundred percent sure what that point was. "The Star of Serendipity is the sister to the Cobalt Star. It's said they came from the same basalt deposit."

I lifted the gem to get a closer look at it. "This is a ruby. The Cobalt is a sapphire."

"A ruby is simply a red sapphire," he said as if I should already know these things. "They're of the same stone. It's their impurities which give them their different colors. Iron and titanium for sapphires, chromium for rubies."

"Huh. I learn something new every day."

"One does hope," he replied dryly. "The Serendipity and the Cobalt are two very beautiful pieces of quality gemstone, but they are not magical. The kobolds only desire the Cobalt Star because it's pretty, shiny, and the perfect shade of blue."

I looked Drake in the eye. "Did you buy the Cobalt Star at Christies, back in the '40s?"

"I tried to," he admitted with a grunt of annoyance. "The Serendipity has been in the family for centuries. It would have been nice to reunite it with the Cobalt Star. But it was a private auction. Closed bids, you know how it goes."

"Yeah, sure."

"Well, I didn't get it," he said as if it was now a closed matter that was never meant to be spoken of ever again. "And at this point, I am of a mind to just give you the Serendipity and wash my hands of this whole mess."

"Wait, wut?"

"Sit." Drake gestured to the chairs as if to command me.

If it wasn't for the fact that I knew Drake (and dragons in general), were like this, then I might have taken it personally. Slapping him across the face was still on the table as well. Saving my life only gave him so much of my good will.

After giving him a suitably annoyed look, I went to sit down. I wasn't completely dry yet, so I took the mostly dry towel and laid it down first. Everything in the room looked old and valuable, and momma did teach me some manners.

Drake gave a very long sigh, sitting across from me. "After the Star was sold, this retrieval spell started popping up, along with renewed interest in combining the Star with the Serendipity and a third gem, a yellow sapphire named the Sun Star."

"There's a third one?"

"Yes, but no one has ever seen it. It may not even exist." Drake looked thoughtfully out the window. "The legend says, if you bring the three gems together, it becomes a considerable source of power. It's just another magic battery myth."

Magic is energy; it cannot be created or destroyed. You use it, you lose it, and you gain it back in the cycle of life. Your aura is where you store that magic, but the raw potential energy of a magic user is almost never fully realized by them. Even my ancestor, First Master, was only able to unlock about two-thirds of his power, and he was stronger than Merlin.

Okay, it depends on who you ask, but he was still pretty darn strong.

Early on in witchcraft, the idea of energy vessels started to form. Putting magic into something and storing it there is easy enough. That's what happened during the Canton incident. The wizard tried to drain Drake Senior's magic into a vessel, to ready it for a one-time-use spell. And that's pretty much how it goes: once you use it, it's gone, back into the cycle.

But what if there were items that could hold massive amounts of magical energy, then naturally refilled themselves? Not items that have spells or their own magic. I'm talking about a vessel specifically designed to hold pure, untouched, distilled magic until you wanted to do something with it. It'd be like a rechargeable battery, only you wouldn't have to plug it into anything. It would pick up magic from the world around it and store it for you, which would give any wizard a distinct advantage.

No one has ever found one. Sure, there are some small scale instances of it found in nature. And I guess I'm technically one—well, all wizards are, but me especially with my special abilities. But even the TechnoMages haven't figure out how to make a magic battery of considerable size work. Something about the magic always becoming unstable and overloading.

So yeah, most wizards simply don't believe they exist, in nature or otherwise.

"You're sure it's a myth?" I had to ask. I mean, I was inclined to believe him, but after everything that happened in the past two days...

Drake gestured to the Serendipity. "Even if the three stones only work together, the individual gems would at least have some trace of the magic that would bind them together. A taste of what they are capable of."

I got the hint and laid my hand over the ruby. Taking a deep breath, I opened my mind's eye and delved deep into the essence of the gem. Peeling off the layer of perception magic created by its value, I found absolutely nothing below. It was a magical void, as one would expect of a non-magical item. No trace nor hint of it being capable of storing magic. I even sent some energy into it, and it just sat there for a moment until finding the path of least resistance: me.

"Okay, I get your point," I said as I released the stone. "Are you sure this is the real Star of Serendipity?"

"Positive," he sharply retorted. "It was proven a long time ago that this is the Serendipity and it has no magic in it. This is why no one—well, relatively few—have ever gone after it. I can only imagine they want the Cobalt Star first to prove legitimacy to the myth."

"Alright." I shrugged as I tried to figure out what he likely wasn't telling me. It's not that I knew he was lying, but it's just… It's Drake. "How did you know about the retrieval spell and the pool portal?"

"We're not calling it a pool portal."

"It almost killed me. I'll call it whatever I want."

Drake rolled his eyes. "As I said, copies of a retrieval spell started to pop up. It's flawed, as you well know. It fails to retrieve the Cobalt Star and instead creates a portal where the caster ends up here. I can only guess this is because the Serendipity acts as some kind of anchor via perception magic created by the myth."

"How have I not heard of this?" Correction. "How has Phil not heard of this? He knows, like, everything."

"It's hard to spread the truth of a dangerous spell when no one survives it," he answered darkly. "It took me years to figure out what was happening. You're the first to live through the trip."

"Oh, ah, yay me?"

"However Mr. McCree came across the spell, it's a fool's errand," Drake dismissed the whole affair. "I will put you up tonight, but tomorrow it's through the nearest shadow gate back to New York with you, where I hope you will shred that spell before anyone else gets hurt."

I was busy thinking and only really comprehended half of what he just said. "We didn't find the spell. It was brought to us by a non-magic user. He only had it because he was tasked by a fae to find it."

Drake tilted his head, pinching his brow. "Which fae?"

Well, there was nothing to lose at this point. "Avalbane. She tasked a college professor from Dover, Delaware— Yeah, you remember Dover, don't you?"

He gave me a dismissive gesture with his hand.

"Anyway," I continued. "She promised him a life without wanting if he brought her the Cobalt Star. The thing is, there were no caveats or conditions."

"That does not sound like a fae."

"Yes, we've established that." Okay, so he wasn't there when we did, but still. "Do you know Avalbane?"

"I know of her," Drake admitted. He does live in Wales, so I wouldn't have been terribly surprised if he said something like she was his neighbor. "She's very crafty."

"Phil said she was low-level."

"She would like people to think that." Drake laughed dismissively. "Avalbane is not like many of her kin. She is more than happy to work in shadows and keep her name out of things. The fact that she did not put a caveat on her request is highly suspect."

Suspect indeed, but it wasn't like I could just call Avalbane and ask her what she's up to. For one, fae don't have phones, but mostly, you can't trust them. Just asking a simple question could end up with you having to give them your firstborn.

Drake put his hands together as he sat up straight in his chair. "This just reiterates how much trouble the Cobalt Star is. When you return tomorrow, make sure Phil destroys the spell."

"It will be strongly discussed," I replied, then it clicked. "Shit. I'm going to be stuck here overnight."

"I promise you, I am far more put out," Drake said drolly. "I will be having several dinner guests. It's a black-tie affair. If you would be so kind as to stay in your room, I will have food brought to you by one of my servants who will keep you company in case your lungs start filling with water, or something."

"You'll all heart," was what I would have said, but instead them words were spoken by a new arrival to the parlor.

A woman with pure alabaster skin and flowy silver hair walked into the room. Her heels clacked with dominance on the wood floor, her stride sure and purposeful. She wore a long black skirt and intricate silk top that looked like it was worth more than the gross national product of a small country.

She stopped mere feet from me, taking in my drowned rat appearance while addressing Drake. "So, this is her."

"Yes," Drake replied in a very even tone. "This is Miss Dominque Masterson."

"Nevina Argent," she said in her far more posh sounding accent as she held out her hand. "You can call me Nev. I've heard a lot about you, Miss Masterson."

"That always sounds ominous," I mumbled as I shook her hand, her nails a chrome silver. "You can call me Minni."

"Cute." She seemed to genuinely think so.

It took me a second to realize her pale blue eyes were a glistening silver color. Even her skin had something of a sheen to it. "You're a silver dragon."

"Oh, my word, how did you know?" Nev gave me a rather faked look of surprise.

"The poor woman nearly drowned mere moments ago." Drake stood from his chair. "You're early."

"I wanted to give myself plenty of time to get ready," Nev replied with a bit of a pout. "This is a new form. Most of our guests won't have seen it yet."

"Of course, of course," he quickly responded and then looked like he was trying to inch towards the door. "I offered Miss Masterson some of your old clothes. I hope you don't mind."

"Don't mind at all." Nev turned to me and smiled. "Come on, I'll help you pick something out."

"Thanks," I said cautiously, standing. I wasn't sure if I should be gracious or terrified. I settled on something in between as I felt the weight of Serendipity on my neck. "We should probably put this back."

"Keep it," Drake told me and I think I stopped breathing for a good five minutes. "At least until I decide what I want to do with it. I am getting extremely tired of all the bodies piling up."

"Aiden," Nev tsked as she started to walk me out of the room. "That's not something a lady wants to hear when you give her jewelry." She glanced down at me. "Well, not these days anyway."

Ugh, *dragons*.

The entire walk up to the guest room, I thought about Marcel. I couldn't text him, couldn't call him. I mean, I could borrow a phone but how was I supposed to explain a British number on his caller ID?

I also had no idea how I'd explain being gone all night either. I hoped maybe Drake wouldn't be a stickler for an actual twenty-four hour turn around. If I made it through the night, got up early, then with the time change I could be back in New York at like, one in the morning. Marcel would still be up, probably.

"Here we go." Nev gestured to the open door of one of the many rooms on the second floor.

Nev let me go in first and I was greeted by a woman not much older than me. She had on a white and gray maid's uniform and was smoothing out several pieces of clothing on the bed. I don't know what I was expecting of the room itself, perhaps something dark and gothic, opulent. Instead, I was assaulted by a small room decorated in pastels… turquoise pastels with little rosettes on the wallpaper.

And paisley. Lots of paisley.

"Ma'am." The maid backed away from the bed and bowed slightly, but I wasn't sure if it she was addressing me or Nev.

"Is the en suite stocked with toiletries?" Nev asked her.

"Yes, ma'am."

"Excellent." Nev turned to me, her nose wrinkled. "You smell like a bad bleach job. You'll want to shower first."

So, dragons apparently have a high sense of smell. Good to know, maybe. I don't even know why I bother to mentally catalogue any of these things. Maybe because I could smell the chlorine too, always been able to. Everyone else thinks I'm crazy though. I mean, I probably am, but for many reasons not related to my sense of smell.

The maid piped in. "I'll launder your clothes right away, ma'am."

"Thanks, uh…"

"Lucy."

"Lucy, call me Minni." I felt a bit uncomfortable. I'd never had a maid or someone waiting on me like that. I guess I was supposed to feel pampered or something. "Uh, let me just pick out a shirt and pants to change into."

Lucy gestured to a pile of silk and lace sitting at the foot of the bed. "I've selected some new undergarments for you as well."

Nev lightly laughed. "I have a horrible tendency to just buy things and never wear them."

"Must be nice," I mumbled, picking up a green top to check the label for the size. "Is this a real Alexander McQueen?"

"If that's what it says." Nev moved over to a corner chair and made herself comfortable. "Take whatever you like. This was all from my previous form. I've already stocked my closet with new clothing for this form."

"Form?" I absently asked as I looked through the clothes. They were all expensive labels from fashion designers I had actually heard of. I was going to steal all of them. Not for me, of course, for Stacey. She wants to be the next Alexander McQueen. She'd have a field day with all this.

"I had to return to my true self a few years back," Nev explained as I half listened. "I was only able to change into a human form a month ago. My proportions are not the same, and I prefer tailor fits."

I set down the Elle Saab I was holding and looked over at Nev. "You are horribly one-percent, you know that, right?"

Nev gave a dismissive tsk. "Don't lump me in with those bourgeois bottom feeders."

I turned to Lucy. "I hope they're paying you well."

"Extremely," Lucy smiled. "I just bought a Maserati."

"Nice." I was too tired to deal with the surreal nature of what was going on. After grabbing the closest thing I could find to a t-shirt, some yoga pants, and undies, I walked to the bathroom.

Nev called out. "Aren't you curious, about everything going on right now? The party, the clothes? Me?"

"Nope." I looked for a place to put everything as it was a small bathroom. I settled on the lid of the closed toilet as there was no counter space.

"Not even a little bit?" She now stood in the doorway. "You have a rare look into the dragonkin community. Gaerwen was said to be very curious."

I was waiting for when my great something-infinity uncle Gaerwen was going to get brought up. Long story short, he wrote a definitive encyclopedia on dragons way back when. It ended up getting used against dragons by a corrupt king years later.

It was another great-uncle from different branch of the Masterson family who stopped the king and destroyed the book. We don't have an actual name for him. He's only known as the Copper Knight.

"Unlike my ancestors, I really don't care about dragons." I grabbed the edge of the door. "In fact, I don't even like them."

"Is that so?" Nev looked like she was trying not to laugh. "You should hold onto that feeling."

I swung the door shut in her face. Yeah, I am totally stealing all her clothes.

As I started to get undressed, I realized I was still wearing the Star of Serendipity. At first I thought I'd take it back into the bedroom, but worried what would happen if it went missing. Not that I thought Lucy would take it, but possibly Nev might if she wanted to mess with me. She was being real weird towards me. I also wasn't going to leave it on top of the toilet or the edge of the sink. Even though there was no way for the ruby to go down the drain, I couldn't help but feel a little anxiety about it.

Do you know how much that thing is worth?

Okay, so I don't either, but that just made it worse because I imagined quite a bit. I ended up showering with it on, because, I dunno, reasons? Leave me alone. It's been a weird couple of days.

I got washed, dried, and dressed in record time. I found Lucy waiting for me in the bedroom. Nev's clothes were gone, but there were a few large tote bags by the door.

"I packed up everything for you," Lucy said. "I assumed you were taking it all."

"I like you."

"I'm good at my job." She winked and then turned, picking up a phone from the dressing table. "Mr. Drake has replaced your phone for you. Your sim card has already been transferred. Your old phone is currently sitting in a bowl of rice in the kitchen."

"Uh, thanks." I really hate it when dragons are nice to me. It makes me so paranoid.

"Mr. Drake also wanted me to point out that this model is both waterproof and shatterproof."

"Because of course it is." I stared at the expensive piece of equipment, the Serendipity reflecting in the black screen. "I didn't die in the pool, did I? And this is some kind of purgatory?"

"I couldn't say, ma'am."

"That's not a no…"

EIGHT[8]

First thing I did was text Marcel and apologize, telling him I'd be late. Honestly, I don't know why he puts up with my flaky ass. He really deserves better.

We texted back and forth as I called Phil and filled him in on what Drake told me about the Cobalt Star and the Star of Serendipity. I still hadn't taken it off. I would teeter back and forth between anxiety and absolute fabulousness because how often does one get to wear expensive jewelry like that?

"This feels like too much of a coincidence," Phil said as the line crackled.

"Yeah," I agreed as I sat on the bed, propped up with like a dozen little pillows. "Drake causes a rift in Dover, then a person from Dover comes looking for a necklace he has the twin of? And that person is also Welsh? My head is spinning."

"Speaking of, you doing okay?"

"Other than being stuck here and not with Marcel? I'm fine. I wasn't in the water very long."

"Good thing Drake was there." Phil seemed like he was happy but there was an underlying note of something in his voice. It would have been a good time to ask him about the call history on Drake's phone, but, per usual, I was a little too self-absorbed to remember. "Anyway, you rest up. Ryan and I are looking into the spell. We'll see if we can't figure out what's wrong with it. Harper is talking to a Forsaken in the Dover police department about Perkins."

"Alright, have fun?"

There wasn't much left for us to talk about, so I let Phil go and do his thing. Then I got another text from Marcel, this one a simple: *Peek-a-boo*.

It made me smile and feel like he wasn't thousands of miles away. I texted back with: *I see you.*

God, I love him.

Right, sorry. Pixies, kobolds, dragons, oh my.

So, Lucy would come up and check on me about every half hour. She was helping to prepare things for the party Drake was having. Apparently, he does this a few times a year. He invites a lot of dragon big wigs to his place to remind them who's the boss. According to Lucy, this one was not exactly scheduled and put together at last minute a few weeks ago.

I admit, I was a little curious about that, especially since it's possible one or more dragons may have been involved in his father's kidnapping and attempted murder. But I had no desire to get involved in that kind of drama because I'm sure dragon drama is hella dramatic.

Lucy had checked on me and left again when I noticed car lights outside the window. I peeked out from behind the paisley curtains to see several very fancy cars pull up to the house—I was in a room towards the front end. Men and women clad in tuxedos and evening dresses were shown inside. It took me a minute to realize they were all dragons in human form.

Out of a stretched limo arrived two pairs of dragons. The men looked like they could be twins, except one was black as coal and the other so white he was near translucent. I think they were carbon dragons because a little baby dragon seemingly made of charcoal exited after them. It left little sooty footprints along the stone pathway that disappeared only moments later. It bounced around like an excited puppy.

No lie, it was adorable.

I couldn't recognize all the elements as a lot of them were about the same alabaster color as Nev. I doubted they were all Silver. I figured the others were probably different gray-ish colored elements, like platinum or mercury. I'm not even sure how many different elemental dragons there are.

Someone, I think Ryan, once commented that there were, at least at some point, a dragon for every element on the periodic table. I thought that was kind of ridiculous. I mean, just how would a xenon dragon work? Or an einsteinium dragon?

I know, I could have just asked Drake or Nev for answers but I wasn't going to give either of them the satisfaction.

Oh, so I did see what could only be a bismuth dragon. Her skin was black with a bluish tint to it, at least in the light of the driveway lanterns. But her hair, it was amazing! All different metallic colors that were so vivid and bright, cascading around her in multicolored waves. It was so perfect that one would almost have to assume it was a wig.

She was walking up the path when another dragon got right in my face, literally.

"YOU!" I yelled at the actual *dragon* dragon who had moved in front of the window. Oh, I'd know that knobby face anywhere. "Don't think I haven't forgiven you for using me as a bowling ball!"

Ignatius laughed. That's the only way I could interpret the sound that came out of his throat. I'm not up on my Draconic. I was kind of hoping I'd never see another dragon ever again.

"Yeah, uh huh." I pretended I knew what he said. "Come in here and say that to my face."

Don't ask me why I was antagonizing a dragon in his own home. I don't have an answer.

Ignatius huffed so hard he completely fogged up the window. Once it cleared, he was gone.

There was a knock on the door; it was Lucy with a tray of food. "My services are no longer required downstairs," she told me as she sat the tray on the foot of the bed. "I have been asked to keep you company for the rest of the night."

"You mean keep me from crashing the party?" I only half-joked.

"It is preferred if you stayed upstairs, yes," she admitted easily. "It's a private party, and to be perfectly honest, it will be very boring. They just stand around and talk about geosciences and the gold standard, and they gossip worse than a bunch of old biddies."

"Did I mention I like you?" I said as I perused my dinner options. Smoked meats, cheeses, things I couldn't recognize, and even a few chocolate covered strawberries.

"Believe it or not, but our family values honesty."

I literally paused halfway through biting into a crabmeat covered cracker. "Fam'ly?"

"Yes, Ignatius Drake is my great-great-grandfather." Lucy laughed as she uncapped a bottle of fancy water and handed it to me. "My great-great-grandmother was a mortal that Ignatius knocked up. He was, of course, in a human form at the time. They had a son, my great-grandfather. You can figure out the genealogy from there."

"Humans and dragons can have kids?"

"I just said that."

"Sorry." I tried to wrap my head around this. "So, you're like, one-sixteenths dragon?"

"Oh, no, I'm wholly human," she explained. "The dragon DNA doesn't exactly bridge."

"Huh." I'll admit, I did learn a lot of interesting things this weekend. "Wait, so, Ignatius keeps his great-great-granddaughter around as a servant?"

"Dragonkin are very protective of their own, but human offspring are not really considered *their own*." There was far too much familiarity in her words. "Ignatius couldn't treat his son as an equal to his dragonborn, but he didn't want to just abandon him. So, Ignatius justified giving his son a relative fortune by taking him on as a servant. Then it kind of became a family thing, and we are paid *extremely* well for our time in service to the Drakes. Did I mention I just bought a Maserati? A convertible. I'm taking a driving tour of the continent in the spring."

I honestly didn't know how to process what she was saying. I mean, she seemed happy and who wouldn't want to be able to afford a fancy car and a driving tour vacation? I can barely afford my apartment some days. But still, how could Ignatius do this? Lucy was his great-great-granddaughter, and she's Aiden's grandniece, or great-grandniece, whichever.

"You're his family…"

"Here." Lucy handed me another crabmeat cracker. "Don't think about it too hard."

I shoved the food into my mouth and decided that none of this was my business.

We sat down to dinner and Lucy told me all about the trip she was taking. Two months, *two months*, she would be travelling to nearly every country in Europe with her sorta/kinda fiancée. Lucy had it all planned out on a spreadsheet and everything. She already started booking hotels and events. It was like an extended two-year anniversary slash birthday gift for her girlfriend.

It's women like her that really put me to shame.

We should take a trip sometime. I texted Marcel. *Just me, you, no phones, and a cabin in the woods. No distractions, just peace and quiet.*

You realize you said 'cabin in the woods,' right?

*I do now. *facepalm**

As Marcel got a good laugh out of me for the next half hour, I also had an awkward conversation with Lucy. She asked if I enjoyed my Thanksgiving. I explained I didn't celebrate because I'm Cheyenne. She thought I was Mexican. You know how it is.

I also got the occasional text from Harper, updating me on what was happening back at the shop. I felt kind of bad for hanging out in an English manor house, eating expensive food, and doing jack-all while they worked on solving the mystery.

But only a little.

"I think I'm going to turn in," I eventually told Lucy. I should have been wide awake, after all, it was only five o'clock according to my body, but I was exhausted. And the sooner I went to bed, the earlier I could get up and back to Marcel. "You're not going to sleep in here with me, are you?"

"No, ma'am." Lucy gathered our trash and the dinner tray. "I will check on you before I turn in, but I believe you are now out of the woods, as it were. The doctor was more worried about air pressurization on the lungs right after a trauma."

"I appreciate the concern." As inconvenient as it was.

"There are pajamas in the second drawer of the dresser." Lucy made her way to the door. I moved to help but she expertly opened it while balancing the large tray. "Have a good night."

"You too."

Once she was gone, I dragged myself off the bed and went over to the dresser. Sure enough, I found a couple pairs of PJs, from satin to flannel. I grabbed the flannel and headed back to the bed. As I was about to change, I realized I was still wearing the Star of Serendipity. I don't know how I could forget such a thing, but apparently I can.

What I absolutely couldn't do was sleep in it. I mean, I sleep with my copper foci on, but I've had years of experience with it and it has rounded edges. The Serendipity? Yeah, I'd probably cut myself on a diamond, bleed to death or something.

The whole thing was ridiculous.

Opening the door just a crack, I saw that the hallway was empty. I slowly snuck out and then chastised myself for being so silly. I wasn't a prisoner, nor hiding from anything. Drake simply wanted me out of the way while he wined and dined his fellow snobby dragons.

I headed to the stairwell and figured as long that as I didn't purposefully interrupt the soiree, then I could go wherever I wanted. Or at least where I was already invited into. I mean, I'm not going to be rude and just start rummaging through Drake's sock drawer or something. That would actually be the worst idea I have ever come up with, and I've made a many of questionable decisions in my life.

Descending the stairs, I paused as the bismuth dragon walked by below. She was even more fabulous up close, her coloring practically radiating it was so vibrant. My eyes tracked to the dragon she was talking to. His hair was a rusty color, his skin reminded me of weathered tin siding. And yeah, Bismuth may have been pretty fab, but the Tin Man… holy hell. There was just something about him that made me seriously reconsider my hatred of dragons and men with overly broad shoulders and facial hair…

They disappeared as quickly as I saw them, and we are never to mention this to Marcel, ever. Not that you would ever meet him, but I'm just saying, should on the off chance you do… and I'm going to shut up now.

Collecting myself, I managed to walk to the bottom of the stairs without tripping. The sounds of the dinner party, and Tin Man, were the opposite direction of where I wanted to go, so that was good. I made my way down the hall towards the parlor. The door was open and I carefully peeked inside. Finding the room empty, I went to the porcelain bust that was the home of the Serendipity. I opened the glass case, making sure I didn't shake the cabinet and knock anything over because ain't no way was I going to be able to buy it if I broke it.

My hands went to the clasp of the necklace and fumbled.

"Rude," a voice boomed. I jumped, lifting my arm, the sigil on my bracelet glowing.

"Damnit, Drake!" I lowered my hand and withdrew the energy from my foci once I realized who it was. He walked into the room dressed in a double-breasted tuxedo, glass of red wine in hand. I glared at him. "Don't sneak up on people like that! It's a good way to get a bolt of lightning up your ass."

"Gold *is* an excellent conductor," he said just to annoy me, smirking too. He eyed the opened cabinet. "You're returning the Star of Serendipity?"

"You never actually confirmed what you were doing with it." I went back to trying to get the clasp undone but I swear it was welded shut or something. "I'm going to bed and I don't want to be responsible for it while I'm asleep. It's worth more than I am."

"Never underestimate your value." I think it was more of a personal mantra than an actual attempt to make me feel better.

"Whatever." Yep, the clasp was welded shut, I'm sure of it.

Nev walked into the room, dressed in a dark green evening gown to match the diamond and emerald jewelry that adorned her neck, ears, and wrists. Not going to lie, I was completely jealous of just how elegant she looked, with her silver hair done up like classic Hollywood royalty.

"What did I miss?" she asked.

"Miss Masterson was attempting to stealthily return the Star of Serendipity."

"Rude."

I gave up on the necklace. "I hate you both."

Drake's phone went off, saving me from further comment. He pulled it from his pocket with his free hand, frowning at the screen. He swiped and then hit a button. "You're on speaker."

"Is Minni there?" It was Phil.

"I'm here," I answered, albeit confused as to how Phil had Drake's number. I don't even have Drake's number. Although, I don't actually want Drake's number.

"You didn't answer your phone," Phil said.

"I left it upstairs, sorry."

"I needed to speak to both of you, anyway." There was a light static on the line. "I figured out the spell."

"The spell?"

"The retrieval spell for the Cobalt Star," Phil explained. "Someone took the original spell and made some ingenious substitutions. That's why it looks completely legit."

"Makes sense," Drake said with an approving nod of his head. "And it's likely why I keep ending up with the trash."

"They were people," I told him very pointedly.

"I like her." Nev took Drake's glass and walked over to lean against a bureau, sipping on the stolen wine.

Phil was completely oblivious to all of this. "I figured out the substitutions."

"What?" Drake and I both said. Drake added, "How?"

"Research," Phil spoke the word as if he was offended Drake had even asked. You notice I didn't question it. "We've been at it for a couple of hours now. Putting together all the pieces about the kobolds, the history of the Star, the other Stars, using some good ol' magic know-how... I just had to find the one piece that fit and the rest fell into place."

"Awesome possum," is all I had to say about that. Every wizard has their own specialty: mine is energy transference, of course. But for Phil, his specialty is just *everything*. He knows how to get magic shit done. That's how he became the defacto leader of our group. I mean, we call ourselves a coven, but really we're just a Magical Janitors Union.

"I want to try the spell again," Phil continued. "But it has an ingredient I can't get. I was hoping you could help me, Drake."

"How so?" he asked.

"I need Blue Blood."

"And you think I have some just lying around?" Drake said and Nev snickered into her wine glass.

"Not really, but you'll have an easier time sourcing it."

"Fair," Drake easily agreed. "How much do you need?"

"Not much. Uh, a small test tube if you can manage it?"

"I can have it for you tomorrow."

"Oh, ah, thanks." I don't think Phil was expecting such a quick turnaround.

"I will send it back with Miss Masterson," Drake clarified.

"Good, good." It suddenly grew awkward and I'm not entirely sure why. "Well, I'll talk to you both, tomorrow then."

"Night, Phil," I said. He was able to return the sentiment before Drake cut the call.

"Blue Blood, huh?" Nev pushed off the bureau. "Have fun with that." With a slightly dismissive wave, she walked out.

"So, uh…" Okay, curiosity got the better of me. "Is she your sister? I mean, can gold and silver dragons even be related?"

"Yes, they can," Drake answered as he put away his phone. "And no, she isn't. Turn around."

"Huh?" I blanked, he gestured to his neck. "Oh, right."

I turned around and Drake undid the clasp in one smooth motion. I'm still fairly certain it had been welded shut though. But anyway, he took the Star of Serendipity and placed it back on the porcelain bust.

Maybe it was because I was tired, but I decided to call Drake out on something that had been bothering me. "Hey, does this little party have anything to do with your dad getting bound and nearly killed two months ago?

"Tangentially," he casually intoned, closing the cabinet.

"I know we made it even, but I almost died on more than one occasion that weekend." It was starting to become a very bad habit. I'm wondering if dragons are just bad for my health. "I think you owe me a few answers as to why."

Drake took a moment. I could see his reflection in the glass, all pensive and thoughtful. "Are you absolutely sure there was another dragon in New York at the time?"

"I… I can't be *positive*, no." I ran through all the evidence. "The damage to the lighthouse could have been done by any three-clawed creature. And the double energy signature, well, you haven't given me an alternative as to what other being might present that. If there are none, then it had to be a dragon."

"The energy signature." Drake turned around quickly. "Would you be able to recognize it if you saw it again?"

"Sorry, no. It and Ignatius looked exactly the same." I gave an unfortunate shrug. "The only reason I found Ignatius on the first try was because of where he was, and that little trace of your magic left in me tugged at him."

He tilted his head to the side. "Did you ever get rid of that?"

"Tried to." It's been a slightly annoying point of contention for me. "There's a small bit of residue of draconic magic in my aura I can't quite get at, like the stain of fruit punch on marble."

"Are you comparing my ancient magic to fruit punch?"

"Yes."

Drake gave me a blank stare, then shook his head. "Get some rest. We leave bright and early to pick up the Blue Blood, so we can be done with this."

"Kay." I figured I had pushed as far as I could and let it be.

Drake walked off and I took a last look at the Serendipity. You know, when I had my previous run in with Drake, I started having dreams. Memories really. It was magic telegraphing its moves, letting me know exactly what I was going to have to do, what I was going to have to risk. And the next time I see Drake, he literally puts destiny in my hands.

Yeah… should have known things were just going to keep getting worse.

There was a light scratching and I got that eerie vibe again, like I was being watched. I slowly turned my head to see two dark figures floating outside the window.

Great, and now the pixies were back.

NINE[9]

My first instinct was to strike out at the pixies with lightning again, but I managed to restrain myself. There were far too many valuable items in that room. Hell, the chairs were probably worth more than I am.

The pixies pressed their noses against the glass, hissing. They looked like the same ones who attacked me earlier in Perkins's car. So yeah, they were pretty pissed once they saw me.

With a shriek, they flew to the side and disappeared.

"Oh, this is going to be bad," I said to myself.

I ran from the room, intent on finding Drake. Instead, I went full tilt into Lucy who was in the hallway. We kind of latched onto each other at the arms and did a one-eighty.

"Pixies!" I shouted before we even stopped spinning.

Lucy's eyes went a little wide. "Pixies? Where?"

"Outside." I pointed to the large window in the parlor. "Where's Drake?"

"He went to join the others on the back lawn." Lucy started moving down the hallway, dragging me with her.

"We should go tell him." Yes, that was my big plan. Let Drake deal with it.

"Bad idea," Lucy said as she opened a closet door and started to rummage. "Too many dragons in one place, they'll all get in on it and burn half the county down."

Considering how just one dragon managed to displace a whole state, I was inclined to believe her.

"Here." Lucy handed me what I at first thought was a paddle. "You know how to use that?"

"To play cricket? No." I twisted my hands around the handle of the cricket bat, giving it a test swing. Lucy continued looking for something and apparently wasn't finding it.

And then the doorbell rang.

Lucy stopped what she was doing and glanced over at me.

I asked, "Can pixies use doorbells?"

We both rushed away from the closet, but as I had no idea where I was going, I followed Lucy. The hallway had a T-junction to an entrance hall where a main flight of stairs climbed to the second floor. A man dressed in a waiter's tux opened the door just as we ran in.

The two pixies dive bombed, knocking the man to the ground. They then shot towards me and I took a swing, but I completely missed and hit paneling instead. It was enough to spook them, and the pixies took off in different directions.

"You get that one," Lucy said as she ran into the side room after a pixie.

My pixie had gone into the hallway, bouncing off the wall a few times as it orientated itself. To be fair, I also slid into the wall as I chased after. I was wearing socks, there was no carpet, and I'm super good at flailing. But I was able to keep an eye on the pixie to see it disappear through an open door.

Instead of doing the reasonable thing and stop outside the room, carefully enter, and do a thorough sweep, I instead barreled right on in. This is what happens when I'm left unsupervised.

The pixie flew right at me, claws extended and screaming bloody murder. Cricket bat in hand, I swung defensively. I didn't really expect to hit anything, just hoped to at least make the thing back off.

I connected with the pixie, more of a wet thud than a sharp crack. The little bundle of anger went flying across the room, right into a gong about the size of a dinner plate. Bouncing off that with a clang, the pixie ricocheted into a rather large and ornate chandelier that was mostly brass piping. Pinging around it like a freaking pin-ball, the pixie then fell, and hit a red-stripped billiard ball on a pool table I only just noticed was there. The pixie kind of body surfed on the ball before falling over, head down in the side pocket.

The look on my face!

Nobody saw this! But I swear it happened! The one time in my life where Entropy does something awesome for me, I have no corroborating evidence! It sucks!

And of course, while I was standing there all slack jawed, the pixie had time to recover. It came flying at me from across the room, but this time to escape rather than attack. My swing failed to connect (probably because I used up all my luck), and the pixie darted into the hallway.

I gave chase, sliding and knocking a picture off the wall. I actually forgot that happened. Drake didn't say anything about it, so I guess it's okay?

As I ran after the pixie, it went back the way it came and flew into the entrance hall. The front door was still open, the waiter sitting on the floor, a bit dazed. I had to hop over his legs which nearly killed me as I had no traction. Thankfully there was a rug in front of the door as I fell against the frame. As I hung there in the threshold, I could see the pixie as it shone in the dark. It darted towards the cars which were parked in rows a little ways from the house.

I took off after it, cricket bat still in hand. The air was cool, a light smell of snow hovering, but it was still too warm for that. I gave myself a little thermal boost, the socks only doing so much to keep my feet warm on the stone path.

The parking area wasn't paved, just a layer of smooth gravel. It crunched under my feet, causing me to skid and nearly plow into a limo. I lost track of the pixie after it rounded a large sedan. I walked more carefully, trying to catch a glint of the light the pixie emitted.

A car door opened and I swung around at the sound. A man wearing a driver's coat half-stood out of a limo. "Woah, are you okay, miss?"

"Get back in the car," I yelled at him.

"You're going to freeze—"

"Pixies!" I spoke more commandingly. "There are pixies on the loose, get back in the damn car."

His eyes went wide and I thought that was in response to me, but yeah, no. There was a sharp thud as the pixie hit me from behind, latching onto my shoulders with both clawed hands. It screeched so loudly into my ear, I dropped the bat and doubled over as I became completely disorientated.

I was about to call down a lightning bolt but remembered the driver. If he hadn't run away, then he'd get fried in an uncontrolled burst. When I glanced up to see if he was still there, I saw something equal parts terrifying and adorable.

The baby carbon dragon was running straight at me like an over excited Great Dane, their wings flapping uselessly in the air as they kicked up gravel. They closed the distance quickly, launching themselves at me. I ducked and screamed as I felt the pixie being ripped from my back, taking part of my shirt—not to mention some hair and skin—with it. I think it hurt less when the pixie was actually trying to kill me.

Standing up, I could feel the warm blood dribbling down my back, soaking into the thin shirt.

As for the baby dragon, they landed several feet away, pixie firmly latched within their jaws. They then proceeded to… play? They treated the pixie like some kind of rope toy, pawing at the creature, shaking it wildly while rolling around in the gravel.

Suitably horrified, I just stared at the scene, hoping the pixie was dead because… Yikes. I could hear crunching noises and little wet squeaks.

The dragon dropped the lifeless pixie at their feet and looked up me with big black puppy dog eyes. They even wagged their tail back and forth as if they were expecting someone to pat them on the head and ask 'who's a good boy?'

All I could say was, "You know what? You do you."

Hey, the pixie attacked me like two and a half times, my sympathy only goes so far.

Remembering Lucy, I picked up the cricket bat and ran towards the house. I saw a faint pixie glow disappear around some large holly bushes that decorated the front lawn. Learning my lesson from before, I slowed down as I got to the edge of the bushes, holding the bat up in defense, ready to swing. As I cautiously rounded the hedge, I could see Lucy backed up against the brick of the house, the pixie bearing down on her.

It began to swoop towards Lucy and I started to run forward so I could knock it away from her. But Lucy raised her arms faster than either the pixie or myself could move. She brought her hands together and a wave of fire shot right at the pixie, engulfing it. It screamed as it flailed about and quickly dropped to the ground like a dead weight.

The air smelled like burnt sugar.

"Damn," I said, staring down at the crispy remains of the creature.

Lucy stepped around the corpse, showing me two small, etched orbs in her hands. "Made from gold dragon gallstones."

"Huh." I honestly had no words by this point. The evening was turning out far more violent than I was expecting. Which, considering I wasn't expecting it at all...

"What about your pixie?"

"Oh, ah, the baby dragon took care of it."

"Ember?" Lucy pinched the bridge of her nose. "There goes trying not to make a mess of things."

I pointed at the charbroiled pixie. "This isn't a mess?"

"*This* is contained!"

Ember ran around the corner with the mangled pixie still latched in their jaws, the tiny creature now missing its wings and a leg. I was like *this close* to throwing up.

"Hey, Ember," Lucy said softly, slowly approaching the baby dragon. "Why don't you give me that nasty old thing, and we'll find some nice tungsten carbide for you to chew on."

Jumping slightly forward and back, Ember wagged their tail and then took off.

"Ember!" Lucy growled as she ran after them. "Come back here!"

I followed, despite my better judgement that told me to sneak back into the house, go up to my room, and pretend that none of this had happened. I ditched the bat so as to not make the dragon think I was attacking them, because I saw how that could turn out. But even as we deftly chased Ember around the lawn decorations, we were no match for their speed.

Rounding the side of the house, there was a stone patio along the back with lanterns strung across to light the area. Drake was talking to the adult carbon dragon twins. Ember bounded around, running in circles before coming to a stop between them.

"Ember!" the near translucent Carbon scolded. He must have been their father. "What do you have there? Spit it out!"

Ember stopped and tossed the remains of the dead pixie at their father's feet. They then dropped their belly to the ground, wagging their tail, wings perked up.

"That is not sanitary!" Father Carbon admonished Ember, whose wings dropped. "What have I told you about putting things in your mouth that you don't know where they've been?"

"Lucy," Drake said. "Please explain."

Clearing her throat, Lucy gave a quick rundown of how the pixies attacked. I just stood there, looking around. I could see Ignatius in the distance, but most of the human form dragons hung out farther down the lawn. Lanterns stretched the whole area and waiters waded in and out of the group. It became obvious to me that we had interrupted a private conversation being made away from the herd.

"It was only the two?" Drake asked for confirmation.

"Yes," Lucy replied.

"It was the same two that attacked me in Manhattan," I added, but Drake tilted his head, his eyes boring into me. I got the hint: drop that subject.

"Aiden, my dear," Nev said as she approached, another dragon at her side. She stopped and wrinkled her nose up at the pixie corpse. "Do I even want to ask?"

Ember began to whine softly, giving their father the puppy dog eyes. Uncle(Assumed) Carbon chuckled, covering his mouth. Some words were tossed back and forth debating whose side of the family Ember gets it from, but my attention was drawn to Nev's companion.

His color was grayer than Nev and his skin ashen, so I don't think he was a silver dragon. I got the feeling he was possibly zinc, though I couldn't tell you why. Maybe it was that underlying blueish tint to the gray?

But that's not what made him stand out to me. Now, all the dragons I've met so far have looked European of some sort. I mean, Drake has a distinctly Spaniard appearance and Nev reads French to me, very Eva Green. This guy? He looked like Daigo Naitō, but with slightly more sensible hair.

I found it interesting. I mean, Zinc had to be a European dragon because he was clearly elemental, and they are the only dragonkin that take *elemental* literally. Nev did say she was in a new form which was different from the last, so I guess dragons can take any features they want. And you know what? He was rocking it. He wore a tux far better than Drake, maybe even better than Marcel, though that is debatable because Marcel... in a suit...

Anyway, this dude was suitably hot.

He also wouldn't stop staring at me.

"I smell copper," he said.

Everyone went quiet and looked at me. I instinctively raised my arms and wrapped my hand around my copper foci. I know dragons apparently have amazing olfactory senses, but metal doesn't technically have a smell. Moving my arms like that did remind me of the dull ache across my shoulder blades from the wounds left by the pixie.

"Oh, yeah." I let out a tired laugh. "I'm kind of bleeding."

Lucy leaned back to get a look at the damage and let out the same sound one would make when they see a man slide down an ice-covered sidewalk and plow into a mailbox.

"It's really just a bad scratch." I played it off because it felt like it had already stopped bleeding.

"Lucy," Drake said. "Please take our guest back to her room and get her fixed up."

"Yes, sir." Lucy gave a slight bow of her head, then lightly tugged me on the shoulder.

As we started to walk off, Zinc continued to stare at me.

"Come, Shirayuki," Nev said as she took Zinc's arm in hers. "We can discuss this with Aiden later." She then proceeded to lead him away from the group in a completely different direction.

Lucy took me back to my room. As I showered—again—she went and grabbed some of this dragon bile balm that Drake used on me back when I lit Phil's bathroom on fire. The fire had given me a really bad sunburn, like the worst, but the balm healed me up in thirty minutes. Lucy applied some butterfly bandages and a thin layer of the bile on the scratches as I sat backwards in a chair, towel clutched to my chest.

"It will suture these scratches and promote the healing process," Lucy told me as she used a bile laced cotton swab on the affected areas. "Try to lay on your front. These deeper cuts will take a little longer, but you'll be completely healed by morning. All considered, you got off lightly. These could have been far deeper and required actual stiches."

"Thanks. I appreciate the help." I continued to sit there staring at paisley as she finished up. "Hey, Lucy."

"Yes?"

"Do you know why all the dragons look at me weird?"

"How so?"

"Drake and Ignatius gave me odd looks when I first met them," I explained. "Like they knew something I didn't. Then Nev asked *is this her* when we met. I thought it was because I saved Ignatius, but then she got way too interested in my thoughts about dragons. And that… um… zinc dragon?"

"Shirayuki."

"Yeah, him. Dude wouldn't take his eyes off me, like he couldn't quite figure where he'd seen me before. I'm noticing a pattern." Especially as the more I thought about it, the more I realized the Carbon Twins looked at me funny after Shirayuki brought attention to me. "Do you know why?"

"I couldn't say, ma'am." Lucy finished up and starting to sort the medical supplies on her tray. "You're a Masterson though, right?"

"Yeah, Sixth Son." I grabbed a pajama button top and pulled it on carefully.

"That's probably it then. Mastersons have been both friend and foe to dragonkin." She tossed all the bloody swabs, my clothes, and her gloves into a small plastic sack. "Wouldn't you look funny if you realized you were talking to a Custer?"

I turned sharply at her. "Custer was never a friend."

"Right, sorry." She blushed and quickly tossed everything onto her tray. "It was the only name I could think of. I don't know much about your history."

"Sounds about right," I grumbled, but I had already ranted enough about that particular subject. "I hear what you're saying. If it makes them feel better, I really don't want anything to do with dragonkin. They have nothing to fear from me."

"I'm sure they understand that." Lucy picked up the tray and gave a slight bob of her head. "I'll let you turn in for the night. I expect Mr. Drake will want you up bright and early."

"You're going to dispose of that properly, right?" I pointed at the sack containing everything I'd bloodied.

"Of course. Straight into a clean fire."

"Great, thanks."

Lucy left and I crawled into bed, sending one last text off to everyone.

I told Harper the truth and I lied to Marcel.

Story of my goddamn life.

TEN[10]

So, bright and early was apparently five am. I didn't complain too much because I got in several hours of sleep, and it also meant it was midnight in New York. It did feel a little weird, with my body clock and all, but I was willing to suffer through it if it meant getting back to Marcel soon.

Lucy had my original clothes from yesterday, washed and pressed and ready to go. Drake insisted that we have a proper breakfast before we left to pick up the Blue Blood. I complained, until I had a plate of bacon, eggs, beans, tomato, sausage, and toast put in front of me. They even put a couple of slices of avocado on my toast. What can I say? I have a weakness, and it is called delicious food-stuffs.

We were sat in a breakfast room, or something. It was off to the side of the kitchen, with a small round table set for four. Nev joined us, so I gathered she stayed the night. As a guest or a *friend*, I didn't care enough to broach the subject.

I was content to ignore both of them, but Nev asked, "Feeling better today?"

"I feel fine… thanks," I answered between bites. The dragon balm did heal me up pretty good.

"Splendid." She smiled, going back to her own breakfast. "Drowning is nasty business."

"Yeah, sure is," I replied awkwardly.

"And pixies," she tsked. "Wretched little things."

"Yup…"

Okay, so: imagine Drake sitting there reading an actual paper while wearing another freaking Henley, like he was god's gift to dragonkin or something. Nev looked like she just stepped out of a fashion show as she pretended to read something on her tablet. She stealthily watched me; don't think I didn't notice. And I was just sitting there, trying to enjoy my avocado toast… it was kind of surreal.

Gold, Silver, and Copper, what with my tinted hair and foci. Three noble metals sit down for breakfast—it's not even the start of a good joke.

It was almost six when we got into Drake's car, his driver quickly getting us on the road.

"Where we headed?" I asked as I tried not to crush my new coat. It was cool during the daytime because it was November in Wales, so Lucy gave me one of Nev's old Chesterfield coats (or that's what she called it anyway). It was long, sleek, soft, and likely worth a few months rent.

Drake was on his phone, sending an email I think. "We're going down to Swansea. There is a royal visiting this weekend. I've sent a request for an audience. The doctor will meet us there."

"And they're just gonna let you take some blood?"

"I will ask nicely," he replied offhandedly.

"Great," I said sarcastically. I leaned against the door and watched the Welsh countryside pass by. Kind of reminded me of the Mid-West. Well, parts of the Mid-West.

It was quiet for a good ten minutes, then Drake said out of the blue, "I would like to apologize for Nevina. She's adjusting to her new form. It's always difficult until the human biology settles down into a baseline."

"Huh." I thought about what he was saying, and it sounded like maybe some kind of biological puberty. I didn't really want to think more on that subject, but it did remind me of what Lucy said last night about human form dragons being able to reproduce across species without complications like sterility. "Does this mean there's a human heart under that golden façade of yours after all?"

Drake looked up from his phone and gave me the most dour expression. "Human heart adjacent."

I couldn't help but chuckle. Drake's still a complete ass, but I guess we all have our moments.

Twenty-ish minutes later and we were pulling up to a hotel that was on the Swansea coast. It looked really nice, swanky even. It didn't surprise me that apparently there was an event happening there that included a member of royalty.

"So, who are we meeting?" I asked as I got out of the car. "Anyone I heard of?"

"Possibly." Drake started walking towards another car. "There are far more princes and princesses floating around than I think anyone truly realizes."

Obviously the more visible a member of royalty is, the more potent their Blue Blood. But we're talking decimals here. The mere act of being born with a title creates a perception filter that marks their blood, but not a lot of spells call for it these days. During the major revolutionary period, wizards developed alternatives, completely negating the need for it. But if Phil said this spell needed Blue Blood, then I wasn't about to argue.

Okay, so, the doctor who treated me earlier was there, waiting for us outside the entrance.

"Did you bring everything?" Drake asked the man.

"As requested."

"Good. Wait downstairs for now. Once we confirm her approval, I will text you."

I looked at Drake. "They haven't approved it yet?"

"I haven't asked," he clarified. "I sent a request this morning for a meeting. Asking them for their blood is something best done in person, don't you think?"

"Point," I begrudgingly agreed. Blue Blood or not, blood is still blood, and it's not something you want to give up easily. I had to hope Drake knew what he was doing, visiting this particular royal.

"Let's get on with it, Miss Masterson." Drake walked off without waiting on me.

I jogged slightly to catch up. "No bodyguard today?"

"I don't need that kind of attention."

A doorman held the front door for us and I immediately felt underdressed with my jeans peeking out from under the fab coat. I also wasn't wearing any make up, although I only wear a little bit for highlights anyway. I take after my mom and the bronze of my skin lets me cheat. Oh, my dad is Irish, hence the copper hair. He's a redhead, mom's a brunette, and genetics are weird.

"This way." Drake veered off to the left and I followed seeing as I had no idea where I was going—something of a theme with me lately. Drake fit in just fine with the surroundings. Still wearing the Henley under a shiny casual blazer which certainly paired nicely with his smug self-importance.

As for the hotel, it was even more fabulous on the inside. The kind of place your parents tell you to put your hands in your pockets. Everything was just so ornate and pretty.

"Miss Masterson." Drake said as I was gawking at some seascape paintings.

"Sorry, yes?" I looked straight forward, sticking my hands in my coat.

"I admit I am curious about your ability to focus energy and lightning," he said we approached a stairwell. "Have you ever tried to use them on a lower level, like a stun?"

"Huh? Um, yeah." I followed him up the carpeted stairs, the wall lined with old photographs of famous people who must have stayed there at some time. "I can create emps, you know that. Hell, I fried your phone that one time, remember?"

"Oh, yes, of course," he spoke in a way that made me believe he hadn't forgotten at all.

"Why the sudden interest?" I asked as we crested the landing, then headed down the hall towards two security guard looking guys standing at a door.

Drake didn't answer me. Instead, he walked up to the guards and announced himself. "Sir Aiden Drake to see the Princess Valerie."

The guard talked into his cuff mic, "I have a Sir Aiden Drake out here, please confirm his appointment."

"You're a Sir?" I asked.

"When I need to be," he replied.

"Understood," the guard said, not looking particularly amenable. "We don't have you scheduled, I'm going to have to ask you to leave."

I frowned. "I thought you sent a request?"

Drake cleared his throat. "Never said it was approved."

Rolling my eyes, I lamented both the waste of time and Drake's pedantic nature. I was very tempted to give him that punch in the face I owed him, right there, in front of the guards.

Drake started to turn to leave, and I followed suit. He used the movement to pivot and turned on his heel, striking out at the guard nearest him. The man only stumbled back. Drake must have not used his full strength, otherwise he would've sent him through the door. Drake instead grabbed a fistful of clothes and threw the guard down the hallway.

The other guard reacted near immediately. He drew a taser gun and brought his own cuff mic to his mouth to call in the attack. Reactively, I reached out and pressed my fist against his chest, sending through a perfectly balanced shock that stunned the guard. He trembled, all his muscles tensing at once, and fell to the floor.

"What did I just do?" I dumbly asked myself.

Drake was already through the door, which I think had been locked, but he just wrenched the knob until it opened. I followed him for a lack of a better idea. Well, I could have turned and ran, but then that would leave Drake unsupervised. I had no idea what his endgame was, and I think that frightened me more than anything else.

Another guard appeared in the entry hall. Drake grabbed the man and threw him against the wall like he was nothing. A second guard already had his taser out and shot at us. I stepped in front of Drake and let the barbs hit me in the arm, through the coat. The resulting shock did absolutely nothing as I absorbed the energy. The man stopped squeezing the trigger and stared at me in disbelief. I grabbed the wires and tugged the taser from his hand.

Drake knocked the man out and moved forward.

"What is going on?" I yelled at him even as I pulled the barbs from the fabric.

Ignoring me, still, he kept going, knocking open a door that led into a bedroom. Another taser went off, but I was stuck behind Drake. The barbs hit him in the chest, the electricity immediately surging into his body. I pressed my hand to his back and, well, like he said, gold is a really good conductor. I took the charge and Drake yanked out the barbs. He then leapt forward and punched the guard who fell to the ground.

"Aiden Drake!" A woman's voice angrily yelled. "What is the meaning of this?!"

Standing in the back of the room was an older woman in a rose dress and a very large flowery hat. She had to have been in her fifties, perhaps older. She was poised, elegant, and fuming in a very murderous way.

"You should have ceded to my request," Drake said in an almost far too calm a voice. "You owe me, Valerie. You could have at least agreed to see me."

"So you thought you'd come in, knock out my guards, and make me?"

"More or less."

"Oh, shit." The full realization of what was happening finally dawned on me. "Is… is this, like, a kidnapping? Are we kidnapping her?"

Drake looked down at me. "More or less."

Yeah, so… *that* happened.

ELEVEN[11]

"I'm dead. I'm dead. I'm going to be dragged to the Tower of London. They're going to chop off my head."

"Do stop babbling," Drake scolded me.

"It is quite annoying, actually," the princess agreed.

"You can't just kidnap someone!" I yelled at Drake.

"Technically this isn't a kidnapping," Drake said, looking to the woman. "It's more of a hostage situation, but if you don't sit down and hear me out, Valerie, then I *will* resort to kidnapping."

"Dead, so dead," I mumbled and started to pace, stepping over the unconscious guard. I found a chair and collapsed into it, leaning forward to put my head between my knees and breathe.

The princess gracefully lifted her finger to point accusingly at Drake. "One of these days these little stunts you pull are going to be the end of you."

"Of course," Drake agreed easily. "But not today."

There was a commotion outside. The guards we knocked out had already recovered and barged into the room.

"Stop, stop." The princess held up her hand. "Stand down. I know this man; I'm in no danger."

"You sure?" one of the guards asked as he warily watched Drake, circling to put himself between the threat and his charge.

"Unfortunately." She heavily sighed, as if this kind of drama wasn't anything new to her. "Stand down, sort yourselves, and find my assistant. Have her bring some tea."

The guard on the floor came to and was helped up by his comrades. No one suffered significant damage, at least nothing that couldn't be slept off. That was by design; Drake's not stupid. The lead guard never took his eyes off Drake, even as we were ushered into the sitting room.

"Let's get something straight," the princess told Drake as we settled around a small table. "I am not doing this for you, but I will hear out this poor woman who you seemed to have dragged into this."

"Thanks?" I really didn't know what else to say, then the assistant appeared with a tray of tea. "Do you... do you have anything stronger?"

The woman nodded and stepped away.

"Now, young lady." The princess got my attention with a swift gesture. "Why did you want to speak to me?"

"Well, not you, specifically, just a member of royalty," I explained as the assistant reappeared. She poured something amber out of a crystal decanter into my tea cup. I raised my hand to stop her as I had meant coffee, but decided the assistant was smarter than I am.

"Why royalty?"

I picked up the cup and tried to hide behind it. "I need Blue Blood. For a spell."

"Oh really?" the woman's voice took a very stern tone, her glaring eyes turning to Drake. "And so this is how you cash in your chip? You want blood, literally?"

"You owe me, Val." Drake was firm. "But even I would not ask of you something so personal. You give your blood freely or not at all. The choice is yours. I only did all this because you wouldn't let me get close enough to ask."

The princess settled her disapproving gaze on Drake. I took that long, tense moment to down the tea, alcohol and all. I'm not sure what burned worse, the hot liquid or the booze.

"And why are you here with him, Miss...?" she asked me and I went completely blank. I may have forgotten my name for a good three seconds.

"Masterson, Minni Masterson." I cleared my throat. "It's a long story."

"Masterson?" she said the word like she was afraid it might bite her. "Son of the First Master, Mastersons?"

"Yeah, Sixth Son of the Master," I clarified, a bit surprised that this woman knew about the First Master. Not a lot of people believe he ever existed, even some of my own family. "We're the ones that ended up in Ireland. My dad's great-great-grandparents came over during the Oklahoma Land Run. We kind of ended up in Nebraska along the way."

"Those are states, correct? Actually, I don't care," she said bluntly. "Please continue explaining about the blood."

I got straight to the point. "We need it for a matter transfer spell to retrieve an artifact."

"What artifact?"

At this point, I wasn't sure how much I could trust the princess. But that was my usual paranoia kicking up. I glanced at Drake and he gave me a subtle nod. He trusted the woman well enough, and I guess that'll all I needed.

"The Cobalt Star," I said and she didn't seem to register the words. Instead, she just looked at me like she was waiting for me to get to the point. "It's a star sapphire that once belonged to the kobolds of Norway. It was kind of stolen back in... I honestly can't remember right now. Anyway, it was sold at auction in the 40s to an unknown buyer."

"And you want to steal it from them?" Well, when she put it that way...

"Someone, possibly the person who bought it, is floating around a fake retrieval spell," I explained. "It's getting people killed. We want to find the Star, who owns it, and stop this from happening again."

"Who is we?" She glanced between Drake and I. "I seriously doubt you meant Aiden here."

"He's helping," I defended him, which, well, it's the truth. "But there are others. My coven leader, Phil, and a Forsaken cop."

The princess leaned back in her chair and got comfortable while still appearing regal. "I think you should start from the beginning."

It was a reasonable request. I mean, I was asking for her to hand over her blood, after all. I couldn't blame her for wanting more details. So I took a deep breath and started with Perkins stumbling into the shop. I was much more concise with telling the story than I've been doing right now, I think. It's hard for me to tell sometimes. I ramble a lot.

She listened intently, albeit passively, until I got to the part about the pool portal. In explaining how Drake got involved, I mentioned Nev.

"Nevina's back?" she interrupted me to ask Drake, her demeanor completely changing. She seemed to be trying not to sit up, to continue to lounge and play it cool.

"She never left," he answered tersely. "But she has again taken a human form."

"Well now, that explains a few things."

"Not as many as you think."

I totally have no idea what they were talking about and I'm pretty okay with that.

"Alright, Minni." The princess sat up straight after giving Drake a long stare down. "I have heard your story. It has an amazing amount of blue in it."

"I know, right?" I mean, it has been a bit much. I'm not imagining this?

"I suppose you're not offering anything in return for my blood?" she asked.

Didn't really think it through that I had no bargaining power here. "Other than knowing you'll help save lives once we can figure out who is putting out those fake transfer spells?"

She gave a light frown, then turned to Drake. "How about I ask for my marker back?"

"No deal," Drake said easily. "Don't want to muddy the waters of consent here."

"Piss," the princess said rather unladylike, unabashedly so. She tapped her fingers on the table for a solid five raps. "Alright, fine, you can have one test tube worth, that is it. And I expect to at least be notified once this is all over. I would like know that giving my blood wasn't a complete waste of time."

"Totally doable," I eagerly agreed.

Drake called in the doctor. He had taken up a game of

cribbage in the lobby while he waited. I have no idea what that is either. In fact, I was pretty much running blind the whole time I was in Wales. It didn't bother me as much as it should have, honestly. I was too busy counting down the hours, hoping to get back to Marcel. He'd gone to bed by this point, texting me goodnight. I could have always showed up and snuggled into bed with him.

"And there we go." The doctor pulled the needle from the princess' arm. He was quick and efficient. Only one stab to hit the vein, a few moments wait, and then he had her bandaged right up. He threw everything into a portable bio-hazard box except for the test tube. That he put into a padded foam sleeve which he placed inside a zip-lock bag.

"Be careful with that," the princess told me as the doctor handed over the blood. "I may not be inclined to give you more if you misplace it."

"Noted, and thanks."

"My pleasure." She was just a tad bit sarcastic with those words. I was really starting to respect her. "As for you, Aiden, next time you deem something important enough to barrel your way through my bodyguards, just tell me so we can avoid the blood on the carpet."

"I told the manager I would pay for that." Drake looked absolutely insulted.

The princess pointed at the door. "Leave, now."

Drake bowed slightly. "Always a pleasure, Valerie."

The two stared at each other. You know that look you give when you want to be angry at someone, but you might also want to throw them on the bed and have your way with them? Yeah, the room got real awkward.

"Okay, thanks, bye," I said and just left.

I was in the hall for only a minute when Drake and the doctor joined me. Drake was entirely too pleased with himself, and it showed through the smug grin on his face.

"Where's the nearest shadow gate?" I asked as we walked down the hall.

"Not entirely sure," he easily admitted. "I have one at my estate. It is a short walk through the Shadow Realm to the gate near the Mercury Shop. I'll give you the directions once we're back and you can be on your way."

"Small miracles," I breathed and checked the time on my phone. It was four am in New York. I wasn't feeling tired but the sudden realization that I should be asleep did make me yawn.

We walked past the manager on the way out. He was not terribly happy with us but hid it well. I'm pretty sure I'm now banned from the hotel for life, and I'm okay with that. Couldn't afford it anyway.

Outside in the parking lot, Drake shook the doctor's hand and thanked him. No discussion of payment was made, but I figure this guy was one of those concierge doctors, seeing as he just showed up on demand. Twice.

"Any place you'd like to stop while you're here?" Drake asked as we headed towards his car.

I think he was just trying to be polite, but all I wanted was to get home. "Yeah, not really. Once I give Phil the Blue Blood, I'm going straight to Marcel's and crashing."

"You're not going to help retrieve the Cobalt Star?"

"I'd rather cuddle with my boyfriend." What? At least I'm honest. "Phil can handle this."

We were like, ten feet from the car when the wind picked up and swirled through the parking lot. A dust devil formed, with me and Drake in the eye. Before either of us had a split second to register what was happening, the world exploded in light. I raised one hand to shield my eyes and held the blood in a death grip with the other.

Everything went calm and silent, so I peeked through my fingers to see... plum trees?

"What the..." I was standing on a path cut through an orchard of plum trees in full bloom. Their white blossoms swayed gently in a breeze against the pink sky. The wind was warm, but not too warm. Temperate. The grass was purple... and glitter literally danced in the air.

"Shit, shit, shit," I swirled around until I saw Drake. I grabbed him by the arm and locked mine around his at the elbow. I tucked the blood into my coat pocket with my free hand, but didn't let go.

"Minni?" Drake raised a brow as he looked at me and our joined arms.

"We're in Fairyland," I nearly shouted, I was that anxious. "I am not getting separated from you. That's how bad shit goes down."

"That's... probably wise."

Fairyland, or Fairy World, whatever you want to call it, is technically part of the Shadow Realm. It's kind of like the major city that's paved over and urbanized the land. The fae had taken over this section of the Shadow Realm and made it their own. Magic doesn't work the same there. In fact, a lot of rules are broken and rewritten inside Fairyland. This makes it far more dangerous than possibly any other realm in existence.

I looked around, keeping watch for any kind of attack. "Do you know where we are?"

"I do believe we are in Avalbane's domain."

"I suppose that makes sense," I agreed with Drake. "She was the one who sent Perkins to us."

"Also, Avalbane means White Orchard." He gestured to the white blossomed trees. "Etymology has its uses."

I have literally lost count of how many punches to the face I owe that man. "I'd tell you to shut up, but I'd rather you tell me how we get out of here."

He thought for a second. "We follow the path. Avalbane brought us here for a reason. We have no hope of leaving until we know what that is."

"Do me a favor, Drake," I said as we moved forward, arm-in-arm. "Never again use the phrase 'no hope' when we're talking about fae."

As we walked, glitter or pixie dust or whatever that stuff was blew around in the wind, getting all over our clothes and in our hair. It didn't look as noticeable on Drake, likely due to his gold hair and complexion, but you'd think I'd just finished a night of clubbing with Stacey. And here, look, there's still some in my hair.

Ugh, *glitter*.

We were in a grove, walking down a slightly sloped footpath framed by plum trees planted in rows. It was near impossible to see past the first line. My eyes kept sliding off the open spaces to fixate on the trees and their beautiful fruit. Eventually I gave up, and just faced forward, ready for an attack if one was to come.

Just as I was about to have enough and start screaming for Avalbane to show herself, the path led into a clearing. In true Wonderland style, there was the most daintily set of tea cups and little cakes sitting upon a doily clad table. Pitchers of cool water glistened and there were Munchkins from Dunkin' Donuts. Seriously, they were in the little carrier boxes and everything. Talk about knowing your audience.

Balanced gracefully on a stool at the end of the table was Avalbane. She was about what you'd expect. Impossibly beautiful, in a flowy gossamer gown of ocher and white that flowed in the breeze—hell, it was the breeze. Her olive skin perfectly matched her ombre hair of burgundy and wine which cascaded from a crown of orange blossoms and blood crystals. And yes, this description is going off the rails but she literally shimmered and I kind of wanted to be her.

"Don't eat anything, don't drink anything," Drake harshly whispered to me as we approached. "Don't agree to anything. Actually, just don't speak."

"I know," I replied through clenched teeth.

"Hello," Avalbane greeted us jovially as we approached. "Please, take a seat, relax. You must be tired and thirsty after everything you've been through."

Drake and I stayed perfectly still. We made sure to stop outside the reach of all the tasty treats so as not to be tempted.

Avalbane gave an exasperated sigh, tsking to herself. "Mortals: you get smarter every century."

I had a really snappy come back but I held it in. I didn't feel like antagonizing her was a good idea at this juncture. Which is amazing since I have a tendency to antagonize everyone I meet.

"Alright," Avalbane was thoroughly put out. "You have to at least listen to me, and then you can go home, yes?"

Silence.

Avalbane rolled her eyes. "Mortals." I'm sure that was meant to illicit a response from Drake who is not, in fact, a mortal. Though it's possible Avalbane didn't know the difference. "I see you're looking for the Cobalt Star, and you're the closest to finding it than anyone else has ever been before. I mean, it's truly commendable. You should be deservedly proud of yourselves."

Nope, not taking that bait either.

"I'd say I'd give you the same deal I gave the other fellow. Bring me the Cobalt Star, I give you a life without wanting. But I don't think that would appeal to either of you. After all," her eyes turned to Drake, "you already have a life without wanting, don't you, my little elemental man?" Getting no rise from Drake, Avalbane looked at me. "As for you, no, you can't be tempted with riches. You wouldn't know what to do with yourself if you had want of nothing. Probably just go mad."

This fae did her research, and I think that scared me more than the prospect of being turned into a toadstool.

"How about this?" Avalbane grinned deviously, steepling her fingers. "I will grant a single favor to whomever brings me the Cobalt Star. I even promise I won't be puckish about it. Whatever you desire, I will make it happen. No strings, and no nasty side effects."

Okay, so, holy shit, right? Avalbane basically offering to give away the nuclear codes to the biggest weapon in her arsenal. Having a fae owe you, and they promised not to be dickish about it, you could literally rule the world if you felt so inclined. By the way I felt Drake suddenly tense and try to control his breathing, he was thinking the same thing I was.

"That's my offer, but it is first come, first serve." Avalbane smiled and glanced between us, likely taking bets with herself as to whom would give in first. "Well, that's really all I had to say. When you find it, speak my name three times and I'll come by and pick up my prize and bestow my marker." She pointed to two larger trees off to the side of the clearing. "Just walk between those, and you'll be back where you're meant to be."

Drake started pulling us towards the exit. Unfortunately, I had reached my daily limit of available survival instinct.

"What is so important about the Cobalt Star?" I asked her, digging in my heels. "Why do you want it so badly?"

Avalbane's eyes lit up and she gleefully patted her hands together. "So glad you asked!"

"Minni," Drake hissed my name.

"I won't bore you with all the little details of the political intrigue," Avalbane started out as if she was gossiping, which she probably was. "Suffice to say, a little war is brewing. The Cobalt Star isn't exactly a lynch pin, but whoever has it has the good graces of the kobolds. And I'm the only one brilliant enough to see just how important that is."

"Were the pixies with you?" I asked.

Avalbane grinned, a dark menacing portrayal of glee that she wore like a finely tailored suit. "Now that, my dear, would be telling you far more than you need to know."

Alright, she had me. I wanted more. I wanted to stay and ask questions and listen to her answers. Thank you, Drake, for having more sense than I did in that moment. He literally dragged me away, near hurling us between the trees, blinding white light engulfing us. As it gave way, we were no longer in the clearing… nor in the parking lot of the hotel.

"Oh, great." I took in the surroundings. It looked like we had been dropped off in another part of Fairyland, but without the sparkle and unexplainable color palette.

"Huh," Drake said as he turned us around. "This way."

We walked though tightly packed but very thin trees. The air was cool and a light haze hung in the air. I really thought we were still in Fairyland, hence me not letting go of Drake until we reached the tree line.

"Home, sweet, home," Drake said drolly, extricating his arm from mine. We were behind Drake's estate house, a long flower garden, dormant for the winter, laid before us. Signs of last night's party were still there in the form of darkened lanterns and lawn furniture. "Nice of her not to drop us at of the North Pole."

"Yeah," I agreed, pulling the Blue Blood vial out of my pocket. I hadn't taken my hand off it the whole time and it didn't look tampered with. I put it back and we walked up the garden path to the patio. "Do you know anything about the war she was talking about?"

"There is *always* a war brewing in the Shadow Realm," Drake was so not impressed. "It's just something for immortals to pass the time with. But it never fails that some unlucky mortal gets caught up in whatever they are fighting over this time."

"This time being the Cobalt Star." I admit I have a limited knowledge of the Fairy World, the Courts, and their socio-political history. So I was willing to trust Drake on this one as it did fit with what I knew.

The back of the house had a large set of French doors I didn't see before. The butler opened them as we approached. "Good to have you back, sir," the man said. "You have a visitor in the salon. Lady Argent is entertaining them."

"Thank you, Gerald." Drake stopped in the doorway. "They will have to wait. Gather Miss Masterson's things, we'll be using the shadow gate shortly."

"Pardon, sir," Gerald interrupted politely, "but the visitor is for both you and the miss. It is a Mr. Thompson, of New York."

"Thompson?" I asked even though I thought 'that can't be right.' "Ryan Thompson?"

"Yes, ma'am."

"Oh, this can't be good," I mumbled and walked into the house, then stopped suddenly. "Which way is the salon?"

Drake was a hundred percent done with me by this point. He brushed past and walked briskly through the house. We ended up in a room just off the front door. It looked like a living room to me. I don't know why they couldn't say living room.

But sure enough, there was Ryan, sitting on the sofa, Nev beside him. She fiddled with something and he was trying to give her directions. They both glanced up when we walked into the room.

"There you are," Ryan said. He didn't look to be relieved or anxious. I took that as a positive sign. "Why are you covered in glitter?"

I pulled at my hair and white sparklies flicker-floated to the ground. My left side, the one latched to Drake, managed to fair better, but there was no getting around the fact I had been glitter-bombed. Drake, on the other hand, looked to have come out unscathed. "How?"

"Trade secret," was his enlightening answer.

"Look," Nev said, holding up a standard padlock. "Ryan is teaching me how to pick a lock. Why, in all my years, have I not learned how to do this?"

"Because if we ran out of things to learn, life would be terribly dull," Drake answered.

Nev gave an agreeing nod, then went back to work on the padlock. It snapped open and her eyes lit up like she was holding the most precious piece of artwork she had ever seen.

"Ryan," I got his attention before he launched into the history of the locking mechanism. It's happened before. "You know I'm always glad to see you, but why are you here? You never get up this early."

"Early?" Ryan frowned. "It was like eight-thirty when I jumped through the shadow gate."

"Eight—what?" I pulled out my phone, I had several texts from Marcel, Stacey, and even Harper. The clock showed that it was two-eighteen pm, local time. "Oh, COME ON!!"

TWELVE[12]

I furiously tapped a text to Marcel, no longer making any pseudo-promises because at this rate I was going to probably end up marooned on a deserted island or something.

"Okay, here's the deal," Ryan started to explain. "Phil and Harper got a lead on who might have poisoned Perkins. They went down to Dover this morning. Oh, with Viv." Vivian is one of our coven members. She's really good with fireballs and offensive spells. "Eli stayed to watch Perkins." Eli is Viv's grandfather, also good with fire. "And Phil sent me here, with this."

Ryan picked up his black athletic bag and pulled out a rolled-up piece of yellowed paper.

"Is that the Cobalt Star spell?" I asked.

"Yep." Ryan unfolded it to show us all the marks and notes Phil had made on it. "We tried calling you this morning and when neither of you answered, Phil scryed you. When he realized you were in Fairyland, he guessed it had something to do with Avalbane."

"Astute observation," Drake said dryly.

"The decision was made to send me here to wait on you, or if you didn't show up in another," he checked his watch, "two hours, I was supposed to see about starting a rescue mission."

"Your driver reported your disappearance," Nev added as she clicked the lock closed and started working on it again. "I wasn't too worried. It happens."

I mean, she's not wrong, but just how often does it happen to Drake for her to be so blasé about it? But that is a question for another day, as the more important one was, "And the spell?"

"Phil didn't know how long he was going to be in Dover," Ryan said. "But if pixies were attacking—oh, they tried to get into the shop again. Then I guess they came here. Nev said there was an incident last night? A baby dragon… ate one?"

"Trust me, not as fun as it sounds." My stomach churned just thinking about it.

"Okay, so. If Avalbane was also getting into things, then Phil thought maybe it was best to get the Cobalt Star locked down as soon as possible and not wait on him."

"You think you can cast that?" I asked non-judgmentally. Ryan's specialty is defeating locks and wards, stuff like that. He's not really advanced in other magics, like transference spells, but he's still a hell of a lot more qualified than me. Drake once called me 'barely a witch' and it galls me to this day that he pretty much hit the mark on that one. I'm *really* good at what I can do, but not much else.

"Yeah, no." Ryan gave me a classic are-you-crazy eyebrow raise. "Phil thought Drake could do it."

"Drake?" I turned to the man. He looked so done with all of this. I wouldn't be surprised if he yelled at us to get off his damned lawn.

Without preamble, he grabbed the spell out of Ryan's hands and scanned over it. There was nothing stopping him from memorizing it and then telling us to go. But I still had the Blue Blood, and I wasn't letting him have it.

Drake looked up from the spell. "This does not bring the Cobalt Star to the caster."

"That was part of the sabotage," Ryan said. "The spell is supposed to take you to the Star."

"Sir." Gerald appeared again like magic. I was beginning to think he *was* magic. But he didn't have the typical markers of a wizard, or even a Forsaken, and I didn't want to be rude and poke around his aura for what else he might be. "Mr. bin Sulayem of Dubai has arrived."

"Lovely." Drake sighed and rolled the paper up, handing it back to Ryan. "Set up the spell in the conservatory. Nev can show you the way. I need to speak with my guest and then I'll join you."

"You'll do it?" Ryan was as surprised as I was.

"That is what I said. Now, give me half an hour."

Drake started to walk away swiftly. I stopped him, grabbing his arm. "You being so keen to help us wouldn't have anything to do with what Avalbane promised?"

He jerked from my grasp. "As tempting as it sounded, I have no desire to deal in favors with the fae. Despite Avalbane's assurances, it cannot end well."

Well, he was right, of course, but being right doesn't mean you're also smart. I mean, seriously, look at me. "Then why are you helping?"

"It's as I said before, wizards have died over this, on my personal property." Drake did not take kindly to my insinuations. "I would like to put an end to all of this and move on with my life."

I didn't have a reply for that, so it was good Drake walked away. I watched him go, wanting to trust him. The problem with Drake is that he's not a bad guy, he's just not a good one either. It's sometimes easy to forget that he's not human and therefore doesn't think the same way we do. You can't just apply conventional wisdom to him.

Lucy said the Drakes value honesty, and now that I really think about it, he's never actually lied to me. That I know of. But he's sure as hell done questionable things, like the suggestion spell on Stacey. It wasn't hard to imagine him tricking us to get his hands on a golden ticket. It's like the story the Copper Knight says: *A good man is simply an evil one who understands that everyone else is important as they are.*

Humans aren't important to dragons. Just look at Lucy.

"This way." Nev walked past with Ryan tagging along. We went all the way to the end of the manor into a humid room full of various plants.

We moved an old wooden table into the middle. Ryan started pulling supplies out of his bag, arranging everything as apparently Phil had instructed. Lucy came by with a lint roller and hair brush. She worked on the coat while I wet-brushed my hair over the downstairs sink. This glitter shit is literally never coming out.

Ryan was finishing up when I came back in. Lucy gave me back the coat, and she had done a pretty good job, but the fabric now looked extra shiny. It wasn't long before Drake decided to join us. His mood hadn't changed.

Taking the paper, Drake looked between the spell and the set up. He grabbed a stone and swapped its place with a piece of graphite. Ryan didn't bother to hide his bitch face at that, mumbling under his breath, "But can you break into Fort Knox?"

"Who is going through the portal?" Drake asked us.

"Me," both Ryan and I said at once.

"I'm staying here," Nev answered dismissively. "Don't get me caught up in your shenanigans."

No one asked her, but okay.

"Stand here, and here," Drake directed us to flank him, not even a foot away. We took our spots and Drake held out his hand. "The blood, please."

"Right." I pulled the bag out of my coat pocket, warily handing it over. There isn't a lot of magic you can perform with Blood Blue, but it's still someone's blood and that holds a lot of power. I didn't really think about it before because Phil would be performing the spell. I could trust him with it. "I'll want any unused blood back to be disposed of properly."

"Of course," he didn't argue. In fact, I'm pretty sure he was expecting me to say that.

Drake took the tube out of the bag and foam sleeve, then with a bit of a wrench, he pulled out the plastic stopper. He poured at least half of the blood into a mortar situated in the middle of the layout. I was kind of impressed at how he managed to not get any blood down the side of the tube, twisting the vial and doing a little tip up at the end. It's an odd skill set to have, but hey, I'm not complaining.

He replaced the stopper on the tube, put it back in the sleeve and baggy, then blindly reached back to hand it to me. I was glad for it not being a bio-hazard.

I slipped it back into my coat pocket, knowing I'd give it to Phil later to take care of. I still have it, and the fact that it survived what happened next is amazing.

"When the portal forms," Drake said, "do not fight it."

"Got it," Ryan replied while I gave a general grunt of acknowledgement.

"Here we go." Drake punched his arms out to get his dress jacket sleeves to ride up, leaving his hands completely free. He calmed himself with a deep breath before speaking the same words Phil had said before. Well, mostly. He spoke in Latin and it all kind of sounds the same to me.

Wind started to kick up, temperatures suddenly in flux as energy was drawn into the spell. Mentally I prepared myself to push Drake out of the way if I had to, if the spell started to fail again. I didn't really feel like taking another spin in the pool portal, but at least I wouldn't be caught off guard this time.

Glittering blues and golds swirled around us. Pressure built up again, only not as oppressive this time. It was more like a wave, something that you could get swept along in. There was a blinding bright light and I brought my hand up to cover my eyes.

"This can't be good," Ryan said beside me.

We were standing in the middle of nowhere. Literally. There were rolling hills with brush, but not a lot of trees. The sun was only just coming up, giving the area a soft glow, the landscape mute and still. The air was chilly, drawing heat away from me.

"Where are we?" Drake turned around, even less happy now. He pulled his phone out of his blazer, then cursed. "Did yours survive?"

"Good question," I reached into my pocket and retrieved my phone. It had restarted, but thanks to it being tied to my magic field, it was basically surge protected. I waited a moment and allowed it to sync with the nearest tower. For a solid minute I began to worry that there wouldn't be one. I got 1G, but it was enough. "GPS says we're several miles southwest of Butte, Montana."

"Is that in the US?" Drake asked.

"Yeah, one of the states that boarder Canada." Okay, so I had to check the map to make sure I was right about that and wasn't confusing Montana with somewhere else. "It looks like the nearest town is… not near at all. There's an interstate we can walk to, but the map isn't showing any cities or towns or even outhouses."

"Why would those show up on a map?"

I gave him my best don't-even-with-me-right-now glares. I thought the joke was funny. "The biggest question is why are we even out here?" I slowly spun, my breath drifting in the air. "I don't see any Cobalt Star. Are you sure you did the spell right?"

"Positive," Drake replied tersely. "Perhaps it was Mr. McCree who was incorrect in his spellwork?"

I snorted. "Yeah, between you and Phil, I'll take Phil any day of the week."

"Guys," Ryan nearly shouted, his voice shaking. "Does anyone else notice how effing cold it is out here, or is that just me?"

Ryan was shaking, his Purgatory hoodie pulled up over his head. It hit me that once the temperature dropped, and I started to lose heat, I automatically began transferring magic into thermal energy to make a nice air cushion around my body. Basically, my survival instinct kicked in.

I checked the phone. It was twelve degrees outside.

"Oh, honey, you gonna die," I said as I slipped off my coat.

"Gee, thanks," Ryan replied, but eagerly let me wrap it around him.

He has a lithe frame so, while not the best fit, the coat did manage to slip on over his clothes. I sent a wave of thermal heat through the fabric, penetrating all the layers of cloth to create insulated pockets of warm air. This is always tricky because you don't want to accidently microwave someone or catch their clothes on fire. I did go ahead and lightly warm his jeans down to his shoes. But there were less layers there. "You're going to lose heat pretty quickly through your legs."

"As long as the core is warm, right?" His teeth were still chattering, but not as badly as before.

Before I could say anything, Drake offered his blazer, holding it out to us.

"Thanks." I was having an odd sense of déjà vu from the night outside Club Paradiso when we first met. I really hoped this didn't mean we were about to be attacked by shadow demons again.

Since Drake is slim, though broad in the shoulders, (because of course he is), I was able to fashion the jacket into a kind of skirt or kilt. I wrapped it around Ryan's hips and legs, buttoning it up as far as it could go. I then tied the arms off to ensure it wouldn't slide down easily.

"When you start to get too cold, let me know," I told him. "I'll blast you with more heat."

"You will be the first to know." He gave me a thumbs up then stuck his hands back in his pockets.

Drake cleared his throat. "Now that we have insured Mr. Thompson's demise is not imminent, we still have the Cobalt Star to locate, not to mention finding some manner of civilization."

"Maybe we should have thought this through," I admitted as I took another look around the landscape. "What was your plan for getting back to England?"

"Wales. And my plan was predicated on finding ourselves inside some kind of home or museum." He seemed annoyed at himself. "Or at least near a natural shadow gate."

The sun was lazily rising because of how far north we were. "Can you call for like a helicopter or something?"

I was being facetious. Drake answered anyway. "I could, but it would take time to source one out here, and then to get them into the air. They can't just appear on command." Drake frowned, brows ever so slightly pinched. "How far away is the highway?"

"Uno momento," I said and checked the map. "An hour-ish, depending on terrain."

Drake considered this for a minute. "We might as well

walk to the highway and get a ride into town. Unless something did go wrong with the spell, then we were brought here for a reason. Perhaps if we ask around, we might find a connection. It could simply be a case of the Earth's natural shift placing us slightly off target."

As plans go, it wasn't too bad. I kind of wished I had Canton's shadow ring. He could open a shadow gate anywhere he wanted to. I think Phil still has it, but it's tuned to Canton's bloodline so, that sucks. I don't even know why I brought it up.

"You think you can make it?" I asked Ryan.

"Can, yes," he answered, teeth chattering. "Will I be happy about it? Probably not."

"I'll buy you a hot chocolate," I promised.

"You will buy *all* of the hot chocolate," he said in dead seriousness.

"Deal. Drake's actually the one doing the buying."

Drake opened his mouth, but as we both stared at him, he decided this was one argument he could let slide. Instead he asked, "Which way to the road?"

I checked out maps again, got my bearings, and pointed us in the right direction. As we started to walk, I noticed a point of interest on the map. "Hold a second."

"What is it?"

"Butte has a World Museum of Mining," I told him as I opened my search menu and typed in star sapphire and Montana.

"And?" Ryan asked.

Drake answered for me. "You usually do not have a world museum of something unless you are heavily involved in that something."

"Oh, right, my brain is like sherbet right now."

A quick scan through the search results, and one very helpful blog post later, I discovered that, "Montana is the only state in the US where you can mine sapphires."

"That does not feel like a coincidence," Drake said what I was thinking.

"There are gold mines all over this area." I kept reading,

clicking through links. "Apparently gold miners back in the day would find these shiny little stones in the runoff."

"I could have told you about the gold mines," Drake spoke like it should have been obvious. "There is one running below us, I can feel the remnants of the tapped veins."

Ryan was suitably impressed. "That is so cool. Can you like, feel gold anywhere?"

"Some, yes," Drake answered, giving Ryan a very suitably stern glare. "And, no."

"I didn't say anything!" Ryan defended himself far too quickly.

"But you were thinking it." Drake dismissed him and uncharacteristically mumbled, "They're always thinking it."

While they had their little back and forth, I remembered the Star of Serendipity and how the broken Cobalt spell hadn't brought me exactly to the Serendipity, only nearby. I had a thought, and it might have been pointless, but at this juncture anything was worth checking out.

I walked back over to where we had appeared. I squatted and placed my hand flat on the cold dirt. Closing my eyes, I opened my third eye and tried to see through the ground into the caverns below us. Like a radar scan, the magic pinged and came back to me.

"Well, how about that…"

THIRTEEN[13]

"What did you find?" Drake asked.

"There's something down there," I said as I tried to get a better idea of what I was looking at. "It's a bubble, or a cage, of magic blocking wards."

"It's a vault," Ryan realized before we did. "Someone put a magic vault in a mine shaft and that's where they're hiding the Cobalt Star."

"This was the closest the spell could get us," Drake said as he stared down into the ground. "We are standing right above it."

"Alright, one mystery solved." I stood, surveying the landscape. The sun was completely up now, but there were still no signs of civilization. "How do we get down there?"

"We find the entrance, of course." Drake took a deep breath, his eyes un-focusing as he concentrated on something.

A long enough pause occurred that I took the opportunity to answer some texts, specifically Marcel's. He was supportive of my need to help a friend, but I know he was disappointed. It looked like my Sunday was going to be shot. I mean, I was in Montana prospecting for gold. Literally. My only hope was that the pixies, kobolds, or fae didn't find us.

On a lark, I looked up cobalt and Montana. "Huh, there is a cobalt mine north west of us."

Ryan frowned. "The Cobalt Star has been under the kobold's noses this whole time? That's just mean."

"This way." Drake started walking off. He does that a lot if you hadn't noticed.

I quickly took a pin of our GPS location, then ran after him. We walked and walked for a good twenty minutes before we cleared a hill and saw the mining facility. It wasn't a very large operation. In fact, I wasn't sure if it was still in use. The buildings were brick warehouses with large multi-paned windows, like they were built before pre-fab was developed.

"Lock is new," Ryan commented as we walked up to the oxidized chain link fence. "So are the cameras."

"What cameras?" I asked, looking up and down.

"Oh, they're there," the kid said through chattering teeth. "Trust me on this."

And I did. Which left us with another question. "Now what? Whoever owns this mine, if they don't already know we're here, they will soon."

"We go in." Drake didn't even take a moment to think it over. "If we wait, then the Cobalt Star will be gone. If we use the spell again we'll be walking into an actual trap."

"It doesn't look like anyone is here," Ryan pointed out the lack of cars and the general quietness of the area. "I can get us past any wards."

"Then I shall be the sword," Drake said as he looked over at me. "You can be my shield."

As accurate as that analogy was, I grumbled, "We'll do this as long as you never say that again."

Drake chuckled lightly.

I took that as a binding agreement.

"Ryan." I pointed at the lock.

"Just blast it, please?" he asked. "My hands are freezing."

Reaching out, Drake grabbed the padlock and wrenched it around to pop the chain that held the gate closed. It swung inward on a metal wheel. After we passed through, I closed it so that from a distance it still looked locked.

Drake took point as we walked past the smallest of three buildings. Glancing in the window, it was an office that had been cleared out years ago, the leftover furniture clearly from the sixties, cracked and chipped. But there were hand prints in the dust, and modern fast food garbage littered around. There was also a large generator with solar panels behind the building. It hummed, powering whatever security system was in place.

"The mine entrance is through there." Drake gestured to a large hanger-bay door in the center of a tall building that was built right into the hillside.

Rail tracks, overgrown with grass, disappeared under the hanger door. A smaller, normal door was off to the side, locked with a simple bolt and padlock. Ryan confirmed there were no wards, which I thought was kind of strange. Drake broke the padlock and we walked inside. It was warmer, but not by much.

The tracks travelled to an opening about the size of a semi-truck in the hill. There was a faded wooden barricade set across the entrance, but it could be easily walked around. Old and rusted equipment sat disused and dead. Except one. A gray block of a machine hummed softly, powered by the solar generator outside. Ventilation looking pipes were attached to it. They went into the mine, bolted to the ceiling.

"What's that for?" I asked myself, out loud.

"It's a gas pump," Drake replied seriously. "It is pumping something out of the mine before it reaches toxic levels."

"Something like what, carbon monoxide?"

"Possibly." He literally sniffed the air. "I do not believe it's a sulfide. Could be radon or cyanide."

"Cyanide!?"

"Could be," Drake reiterated. "There are several different gases that naturally build up in mines and underground tunnels. The mining process can also produce several toxic elements. I would suggest you keep your electricity to yourself for the time being, Miss Masterson. Many of these gases can be flammable, some moreso than others."

"Oh, great." It was not great.

"Time is of the essence." Drake started walking into the mine without stopping to grab a hard hat or anything.

I was not going to go into a mine shaft unequipped. I made sure both me and Ryan had a hard hat taken from a rack next to the entrance. We even threw on some reflective vests that were hanging on hooks. All the equipment looked newer but used, so I figured there had to be a reason for that.

"Check this out." Ryan led me over to a large power panel with one of those big metal switches. It was easy to trace the wires coming off of it. I threw the switch, lights coming on down the tunnel, small safety bulbs dimly illuminating every few feet.

Feeling prepared for our descent, we nodded at each other and walked into the mine. It narrowed to about six feet across, dusty and dank, the ventilation pipes looming over us.

"You sensing anything?" I asked Ryan.

"No, nothing," he answered. "I mean, I can feel the vault in the distance, but there are no wards or traps or nothing."

I was hella confused. "Why would a wizard build a vault and not lay down wards?"

"They wouldn't not do that, right?"

We found Drake waiting impatiently farther in. He took in our appearance and gave us the most 'bless your heart' expression a non-Southern could ever hope to muster. Well, excuse us for not being dragons.

The air was cool, no wind to chill it, but it was decidedly stale. I checked my phone. No signal. I wasn't terribly surprised at this, but now we didn't have our GPS coordinates to follow. As we continued walking, taking a few forks in the road, I trusted that Drake knew where he was going. Like some kind of gold dust bloodhound.

"What is that?" I said as we came to a dead end.

There was a hole in the ground, maybe eight feet wide, the gas ventilation pipes dropping down into it. A piece of machinery, like a conveyor belt, was leaning vertically against one side, disappearing into the depths. Drake wasn't at all concerned. He walked over to the control panel and pressed a green button. The machine started up, rumbling low in the dark below. The belt moved downwards, and every eight feet a flat metal plate went past, going a bit slower than an escalator. I would have thought it some kind of scoop if not for the lack of buckets.

Next to the conveyor was a small platform. Drake walked onto it, then wordlessly stepped to one of the plates as it passed by. He grabbed a strap on the belt to keep himself steady.

"You coming?" he said flippantly as he dropped below the edge.

"That is awesome… and terrifying," Ryan said. "Me next."

"Watch the clothes!" I nearly shouted as he stepped onto the platform to wait for the next plate. Last thing I wanted was to watch a reenactment of a *Final Destination* film.

"Yes, Mother." Ryan grabbed at the jacket around his legs, pulling it out of the way as he took a handhold and stepped onto a plate. He leaned out, ready to meet his doom with a wide grin and super jazzed heart.

I, on the other hand, regretted all the life choices that brought me to this moment.

Taking a couple of short, quick breaths, I let two plates pass before I got the courage to step on one. It felt sturdy: nothing shook or rattled. This did little to calm me as I descended. I dared to take a look down, a faint glow below. It got darker before it got brighter again, the hum of the rotating mechanism echoing off the walls. The ventilation pipe continued beside me. I could reach out and touch it, but dared not to.

Eventually the light grew and I exited out the bottom of the shaft. There was a metal grated platform to step onto, another tunnel opening up in front of me. I nearly jumped off the plate, but it was completely graceful the way I flailed before wobbling into a standing position.

"You okay?" Ryan asked.

"I liked it better when we were kidnapping people."

"Huh?"

I had forgotten to tell him how we acquired the Blue Blood. Been debating if I should fill him in, or just leave it as an inside joke.

The conveyor stopped, Drake at the control panel.

"How do we get back up?" I asked.

"Pressing start down here makes the machine go in the opposite direction," Drake explained.

"Huh, I probably should have asked that question before getting on."

"Yes," Drake said smugly as he walked past.

Ryan gave a disappointing sigh once Drake was several feet away. "Why does someone so hot have to be such an ass? It just ruins it."

I gave Ryan a confused look. "I thought you went for the muscley Jason Momoa types?"

"Did I mention my brain is sherbet? You'll probably start looking good here in a minute."

"Come on." I put my arm around his shoulder and sent some thermal heat into his clothing as we walked down the tunnel. We caught up with Drake who was starting to take it slow on our account. When we felt the outer edge of the vault, we stopped. The tunnel opened into a larger, more brightly lit room, but we were too far away to see many details.

"This isn't a ward," Ryan said as he examined the spell. "I mean, not like something a wizard would do. I think… I think it's a non-dynamic protective spell."

"Then there's an amulet or something in there." Things started to click in place. A non-dynamic spell is one that isn't cast, it's simply there, active, wherever the focus device is. "Whoever's running this operation isn't a wizard, we're going up against a normal person with access to magical items."

"Hardly narrows it down," Drake pointed out with a disinterested flourish. "Everyone has access to magic."

"Technically."

Ryan shook his head and stepped back. "Yeah, I can't defeat this from out here. It's just a magic damping field. It's like a lead box. That's why the portal couldn't take us through."

This slightly horrified me as there was probably a fifty-fifty chance the spell could have simply dematerialized us straight into the rock.

"It only dampens magic," Drake said as he reached out and touched the edge of the barrier. At least that's what I assumed he was doing. I hadn't opened my third eye, and to be honest, I couldn't be bothered. I trusted Ryan's assessment.

"Yeah. We should be safe to walk in and out, we just won't

have access to our magic while we're in there."

"That sucks." I mean, really.

"How encompassing is the spell?" Drake asked Ryan.

Ryan looked a little dumbstruck. "Uh, you can't use fire, but you probably won't be forced back into your true form?"

"Well, no time to dawdle then." Drake straighten himself up and took a breath. With purposeful steps he walked into the affected area. He lifted his hand, flexed his fingers, but at least they didn't turn into claws. Which was good, because as a dragon he would have been trapped down here until we could get someone who could properly enact a shrink spell on a living creature.

So, Phil.

Ryan and I looked at each other, then followed. I could feel the heaviness as we passed through. It really was like a lead weight. If magic was the act of lifting an object, then the dampening spell made my arms feel strained, weak, and useless. I lost my thermal air buffer and it started to get cold, but with little air movement down there, I figured I could last long enough to find the Star and get out.

"It's like I said," Ryan intoned as we walked into the cavern proper. "It's a vault."

Indeed it was. I think the room had started out as a natural cavern that they mined into, going by the way the ceiling didn't look to be chiseled away. Stalagmites—or is stalactites? whichever of those hang from the ceiling—loomed overhead like ever present daggers waiting to drop on our heads. The floor sloped down at the entrance because the whole area had been bulldozed and flattened, though I'm not sure how they got heavy equipment down there to do it. I'm guessing a lot of manual hard labor went into the creation of this vault.

The cavern was at least half a football field wide, with dozens of lights littered across attached to the stalactites. The ventilation pipes weaved around the stone icicles, right into a large, almost air conditioner looking thing bolted to a clear spot on the ceiling. It spouted more pipes off in the other directions. I thought the air would be stale and smell of old dust, instead the scent of aniseed lingered.

Rows upon rows of display stands and antique shelving took up the entire space. Seriously, it was set up like some kind of Smithsonian gallery. Right in front of us were two short pillars, tablets with cuneiform script displayed under glass cases. The closest table had a map under glass on it that looked to be hella old with Spanish writing. In the distance I could see a looming statute of Anubis, represented as a man with a jackal for a head to mimic his dual nature as the Egyptian God of the Dead. Not the kind of thing you want to see loom.

"Why do I feel like Indiana Jones right now?" I said, my voice echoing slightly. "And not in a good way."

"Dude." Ryan freaked. "We find the Ark, I'm bolting."

"Right behind you."

"The Star has to be here somewhere." Drake kept us on point. "Let's fan out and find it before our collector arrives."

"I'll take right." Ryan said, his voice a little more even.

"We're only here for the Star," I reminded him as he walked away. He just kind of waved at me like he wasn't going to not pocket at least one shiny bauble. Hey, I tried. My conscious is clear there.

"I will take left." Drake turned but I stopped him.

"If you find the Star, no calling our mutual friend."

"Fae are not friend," he reminded me. "I have no plans on giving the Star to her. I hope you feel the same."

"I do, but the Star's fate is not exactly in my hands."

"That's not very serendipitous of you."

"Man, I hate you," I muttered as I walked away.

Drake chuckled and I ignored him, looking for the Star. I checked the map display case, finding more maps. I continued down the aisle and up the next, there were a fair bit of jewelry and amulets, but none of it sapphire. There were old pieces of art, from clay to canvas. A few stone statues from nearly every continent. I couldn't really figure out a theme, other than maybe the items were magical and I couldn't tell because of the magic dampener.

"Shit," I said a little too loudly. My voice *really* echoed.

A thought struck me and I immediately went to find Drake. I walked across the back end of the aisles until I got to Anubis. I was going to walk around him, but do you ever get that feeling like you're being watched? I know, it's silly. It's just a statue and it couldn't even use its magic if it had any. I don't care if I sound crazy, but I know it was looking at me. I stared up into its eyes, drawn in gold on the sleek black lacquered surface. It was so weird, but looking at him almost felt like home.

"Minni," Drake shouted and I nearly jumped.

I turned to see him walking towards me from the front of the aisle.

"Found it," he declared with a grin, one hand holding up the Cobalt Star. Even at that distance, I could see it gleam as the light bounced off its polished surface.

"Great." I breathed a sigh of relief that Drake hadn't absconded with it. "But I had a thought, what if these items are being kept here for a reason? Maybe this is a kind of vault for cursed items? The magic dampener isn't to keep people out, but keep these things in?"

"Interesting theory." Drake stopped and took a closer look at the gem. "But the whole time the Star was with the kobolds, nothing happened. Unless the curse was added later."

"Possible," I agreed. My idea wasn't without its flaws. "Let's just be careful when we take it—"

CRACK!

The sound reverberated through the cavern, warping it into something even more sinister than it already was. The front of a wooden display case shattered as a small projectile embedded itself. Drake wore a look of confusion mixed with disappointment as he rocked oddly on his feet. Red began to soak his shirt and he fell to the ground.

FOURTEEN[14]

"DRAKE!" I screamed before his body even hit the dirt.

I started to run forward, but saw them, five men, four with guns aimed in my general direction. I quickly backpedaled, taking refuge behind Anubis. My mind racing and adrenaline spiked, this is usually about the time I start making horrible decisions.

I carefully peered around the statue and easily picked out the boss. He was dressed in an expensive, soft gray suit, his men in black turtlenecks and tactical vests. The Boss reached down to take the Cobalt Star out of Drake's hand. Drake tried to resist, but was ultimately too weak to do so, his head lolling to one side. The shot had been a through-and-through and hadn't killed Drake outright, but that meant nothing if he bled out.

"I will not tell you again, do not shoot unless you have a clear shot," Boss shouted as his men fanned out. He was American, but didn't sound like he was originally from around these parts. He had a west coast accent that was soft. "We don't need a ricochet hitting the air system or any more artifacts."

I glanced up, remembering what Drake said about the pipes having gasses that were possibly flammable. Whatever was in them, it was deadly enough not to risk a puncture. I kept this in mind as my weapon options were limited. I instinctively reached out for my lightning, or just a kinetic shield, but the weight of the dampener meant doing anything with magic would take far more effort and time than I had.

Two of the guards walked purposefully down the aisle towards me, guns drawn but held loosely at the hip. Apparently they didn't think I was much of a threat.

To be fair, they had never met me.

I pulled the hard hat off, throwing it the opposite direction of where I wanted to go. I then darted across to the next aisle, heading towards the area I last saw Ryan.

"Don't lose her," one of the men shouted, followed by the sound of boots thudding on the dirt.

I kept low and ran between several free-standing display cases, the kind that looked like china cabinets with glass doors and oak trim. I zigged around, trying not to give the guards a predictable path to follow. There was a section of tightly packed marble statues, Greek, or maybe Roman. They were yellowed and cracked, arms waving about in a dramatic pose. At least those that still had arms and heads. I was pretty sure I lost the henchmen as I ran through the statues, but that was only half of my problem.

I spotted two different guards, their backs to me as they looked for Ryan. I crouched down behind a large pillar which had a massive vase—Italian, I think—sitting upon it. I checked behind me to see if the first set of men had caught up, but instead my eyes fell on a damaged pike laying on a low table. The bottom half was broken off, leaving about a four-foot section of pitted hardwood. All I saw was a make-shift baseball bat.

A flood of memories assaulted me, of a sunflower field, yellow stained with red.

Keeping low, I moved over to the table and slowly picked up the broken pike, trying not to make any noise. The henchmen moved, but they never turned. I sidestepped to give myself a clear path and plenty of room between the artifact laden pillars. Taking three quick breaths, I started at a dead run.

I struck the man on the right first, swinging with all my strength. The broken piece of pike hit him across the shoulder blade and arm, the force knocking him into a wooden display case that went down under his weight. The crash echoed in the vaulted room, his partner turning and raising his gun. I pivoted on my heels to bring the pike around. I only hit his arm but that's all I needed to do for the moment. The gun flew from his hand.

His weapon gone, he tried to lunge for me. With the broken pike now facing down, I pulled it up so I could drive the smooth end into his stomach. That hurt him enough to stall him, so I kneed him in the balls. He was no longer a threat, but I kicked him in the stomach to make sure he'd go down.

What?

What part of me reads as someone who would fight fair?

"Minni!" My name was quietly exclaimed.

I turned to see Ryan looking up from behind a large metal trunk that may have been on the *Titanic*.

Before I could speak, I could hear the shouts of the other two guards and they were far too close for comfort. I ran towards Ryan, grabbing his arm with my free hand as I went past. Then I set about looking for a better place for us to hide. I found a full-sized Egyptian sarcophagus set upon a carved stone base, winged goddesses holding together the corners. We ducked down behind it, completely out of view.

"Crap, crap, crap." I knocked my head against the base as I tried to get my breathing under control. "I was gonna grab a gun."

"You know how to use one?" Ryan asked, breathless.

"Eh." I teetered my hand. "At least they wouldn't have it."

"I heard a shot," Ryan said timidly, pulling his hard hat off and looking like an extra in an Oliver Twist stage production. "And you screamed. Where's Drake?"

"He was hit." I wasn't going to mince over it, not when our lives were in danger. "It looked bad, like, real bad."

"But, he's a dragon," Ryan reasoned. "Even in human form, they are strong and powerful."

I let out a little laugh. "When your brain thaws out, you will recognize he is so not your type."

I meant it as a joke, some way to defuse the tense situation. That's kind of how I deal with things. But Ryan's voice went small. "I don't want anyone to die... I don't want to die."

I am such a goddamn dumbass.

Ryan is just a kid, well, nineteen, but still a kid compared to the rest of us in the coven. This was not my first brush with death. In fact, I am far too intimate with it. But Phil always kept Ryan back, out of the line of fire. And here we were, staring down mortality with not even our magic at our side.

Dropping the broken pike, I reached over and held both sides of Ryan's face so I could look him straight in the eyes when I said, "You are *not* going to die. You are going to live because you are the most important person in this room."

Ryan was trying not to cry, eyes wide and red. He wanted to argue but I stopped him, pressing my forehead against his.

"Listen to me, Ryan," I said forcefully, willing him to accept my words. "I have a plan. It's insane. It's rash. It's what I do. But no matter what, you are going to walk out of this underground hell and you are going to save lives."

I cheated death once. Not for me, but for my brother. I wouldn't let him die out in that field. So I murdered a man to save his life. Would I murder to protect Ryan? Someone who might as well be my other little brother? Yeah, I sure as hell wasn't going to let him die in some dank underground cavern that smelled of black licorice.

"You can do this," I told him. "You're one of the strongest people I know. I believe in you."

I pulled away and gave Ryan a moment to compose himself. He squeezed his eyes shut, and when he opened them, there was resolve there. The same tenacity that drove him to accept who he was and to leave those who could not. Despite his thievish tendencies, he is one the most honorable and pure of heart people I know. And that was the very reason I wanted to make sure Ryan got out of this unscathed. It was too late for me. I have blood on my hands.

Ryan took a deep breath. "Okay, what's the plan?"

"More of an idea than a plan, but it should work." I laid it out for him as quickly as I could. I'll admit the plan ultimately relied on trusting each other, trusting human nature, and trusting in just a little bit of a luck.

"You ready?" I asked as we heard the jack-booted thugs.

"Close enough," he kind-of-quipped, and I took that as a good sign.

I picked up the broken end of the pike and peeked around the side of the sarcophagus. The coast clear, I gestured for Ryan to follow me as I kept low, speed walking down the aisle of what I realized were Chinese Terracotta Soldiers. Man, there is no rhyme or reason as to how that vault is set up. None that I could see anyway.

I gestured towards the next aisle, trying to make our way around the guards who didn't bother to hide themselves—I mean, why would they? Ryan ditched Drake's jacket so he had complete mobility of his legs. If we could just skirt pass the men and bolt towards the front entrance, then that would have been preferred. But Boss and the two guards I beat up earlier were standing in our way along the wall of the vault in front of the aisles. The man who I had pushed into the display case had a cut above his brow. None of the men looked happy.

I glanced at Ryan who nodded his head, he was ready.

There was a pillar that had some small obsidian orbs sitting on it. There was no label, so I had no idea what they did, if anything at all. I picked up the largest one, tennis-ball sized, then threw it as far as I could across the vault. Breaking glass echoed throughout and we were on the move.

We hid behind a gray, stone obelisk with etchings. It could have come from the Avebury Stone Circle. Actually, it probably did. The guards had moved to follow the sounds of whatever I broke, but not as quickly as we would have liked. They basically hovered about three aisles down from the entrance, blocking our exit unless we could find a way through the antiquities without being spotted.

"Minni." Ryan tugged at my shirt. The other guards were about to walk right into us.

Well, there went Plan A. "Plan B."

I darted out from behind the obelisk, Ryan on my heels, making straight for the entrance. The Boss and guards were in our way, so I came out screaming and swinging the broken pike. I was able to get close enough to take a shot at one of the guards, who was unfortunately smart enough to duck this time.

Ryan tried to run past them but the other guard lunged at him. Ryan jumped back to avoid the man, nearly running into me.

I grabbed a fistful of coat with my free hand and changed his trajectory… to right into the Boss. The two collided with a thump, the larger Boss knocking Ryan to the ground. The guard drew his weapon.

"NO!" I screamed, swinging down at the guard's arm. The gun went off but only after it was pointing at the ground, the bullet kicking up rock. "RUN!"

Ryan was already back on his feet, hauling ass to the entrance. Large arms grabbed me from behind like a vice grip. I kicked up off the ground, planting my feet on the chest of the other guard who had started to train his weapon on me. While I knocked the gunman back, there was nothing I could do to get away from Vice. I tried tucking down so I could flip Vice over me but he held fast.

"After him!" Boss yelled and the two guards who had chased us out of the aisles were already rushing past.

"I'm going to ring this one's neck," Gunman holstered his weapon and looked ready to deliver on his threat.

"No, don't think so," I grunted as I tried to wiggle but damn, Vice was strong. "Not if you want the Cobalt Star back."

"What are you—" Boss started to say as he patted his suit. He turned toward where Ryan and the guards had disappeared through the entrance. "That little thief."

I chuckled in triumph, so Gunman slapped me hard across the face. My lip tore, and my mouth flooded with the metallic taste of blood… like warm copper. I realized Gunman was the guard I had kicked in the gonads earlier. So yeah, I probably had that coming.

The other guards came running back into the vault.

"Well?" Boss nearly shouted at them.

"He got past the barrier," the taller one said. "Threw up a force shield of some kind."

"That's my boy," I said with a proud tsk and grin. "No one can drop a dirty cantrip faster. Get comfy, that thing has a life expectancy of at least three hours. Unless, you know, any of you are wizards."

Everyone glared at me. It's a common enough occurrence. I've gotten used to it.

"Put her down," Boss ordered Vice.

Gunman grabbed the broken end of the pike from me and tossed it to the side. Vice loosened his grip, kicking at the back of my calf so I'd fall to the ground. I planted on all fours, but Vice grabbed my hair and pulled me to sit on my knees. I reached up to claw at his grip, but he grabbed my arm as Tall moved to take hold of the other.

I was stuck, so I took a deep breath and got comfortable. It was only going to get worse from here.

"Wizards, huh?" Boss came around to stand in front of me. "And you're after the Cobalt Star. How clever you must be."

"The fake retrieval spells," I said through bloodied teeth. "Those your doing?"

"My father's idea, actually," Boss spoke proudly. It made sense. He looked like he was born in the '50s, so he couldn't have been the one to buy the Star at Christie's. "The real spell was floating around out there. Flooding the world with the fakes eliminated those who were looking for it."

"But you have the dampener," I pointed out.

"My addition to the family legacy." He talked as if he was a Rockefeller or something. "Beautiful and exotic artifacts from across the world, some as old as civilization itself. All collected here, hidden and protected, for generations to come."

My thought that perhaps this was a protective vault of some kind went up in a puff of smoke. It was just the treasure trove of some rich white guy. "Lame."

Oh, he did not like my unenthusiastic response. I received another slap across the face from Gunman for my trouble. Gave me a bloody nose; damn near broke it. My eyes watered and stung as I was unable to wipe them. I could feel my shirt soaking through with blood, snot, and tears.

"Oh. My. God." I just started laughing. I do that when I roll past fear on the emotional scale. "You are the whitest white rich boy I have ever met."

He was horribly insulted. I could tell by how he gasped and clutched his pearls.

Metaphorically speaking.

FYI, laughing while having a bloody nose isn't the smartest thing. "Seriously, dude, don't make me say it."

Boss frowned at me. "Say what?"

I cleared my throat. *"It belongs in a museum!"*

Well, at least Tall and Vice appreciated my Indian Jones impression, if their chuckle was anything to go by. But I wasn't making any friends with the Boss. He pointedly looked down on me and said. "I should have them put you out of my misery."

"Then you'll never get the Cobalt Star back," I pointed out, unafraid. Okay, a little afraid. "And everyone is going to know about this little vault of yours."

He thought that over for a moment. "You expect your friend to trade the Star and your silence for your life?"

"Honestly, he won't have a chance to," I answered coldly.

"You… are a very confusing young woman." Well, he's not wrong. "What game are you playing here?"

"No game." Because a game assumes there are rules and a semblance of order. "Right now I'll settle for my friend getting out of this with his life," I replied darkly. "And you assholes, y'all getting what's coming to you."

"He won't make it far." Boss was not at all intimidated by me. "Yes, I think I'll just have my men kill you now."

I took a deep breath. "What's in the pipes?"

"The pipes?" Boss instinctively looked up. "Why?"

"Well, if it's really flammable, then we're talking a fiery death. Lots of screaming and smells, I'd imagine. Burnt hair and all that," I said casually. You know, I can be a bit sociopathic when I need to be. Which is troublesome now that I say it out loud. But at the time, I could only focus on what had to be done. "But if it's not flammable, then we're talking slow suffocation… Now that's a terrifying way to go."

Boss stepped forward and grabbed my bloody chin. "What did you do?"

"What *will* I do," I corrected him, grinning through bloodied teeth. "I'm going to throw a lightning bolt up there and see what happens."

He hesitated. "You can't do magic in here."

"Wrong, asshat." My expression may have turned manic, but I was under a lot of stress. "Magic isn't gone, it's just a lot harder to act on."

As I had sat there, stalling, I reached for my magic and it was… so… heavy. But I pushed, and it burned, and I was stubborn. Static started to build across my body, making my hair stick up almost as if I was touching a Van de Graaff generator. This transferred to Vice and Tall who uncomfortably shifted but didn't let go. Boss practically jumped back.

Gunman unholstered his weapon and trained it on me.

"Bad idea," I nearly sang the words. "I lose control and who knows what might be released."

Boss gestured for Gunman to hold. "You won't do it."

"Sonny, you have no idea what I'm capable of."

Sometimes, neither do I.

"You'll die too," Boss pointed out.

"I'm dead either way, so, meh." I managed a small shrug of my shoulders. "And if you're thinking I'm not the kind of person to go through with such a threat, well, let me remind you: there is no such thing as a good man, only an evil one who knows everyone else is just as important as they are." I glanced between all of them. "Almost everyone…"

By this point, I was broken. My metaphysical body was screaming in pain at fighting the dampening spell. I knew that if I did die, I would do so having lied to Ryan. I told him what he needed to hear to get him to leave me and call for help. I told him we'd arrange an exchange and it would be a stalling tactic. But I knew better. These were the kind of men who would have killed us both before help could arrive. So I changed the equation: the guards and I die, Ryan lives.

Boss looked at me strangely. "That quote. That's from *The Copper Knight*."

"Fuck you." I spat blood at him. "That story is my family's. You can't have it."

"You're a Masterson, then." He didn't question it. "I don't think you'll be missed."

"Eh." I shrugged and then grinned, congealed blood dripping slowly down my chin. "Will you be?"

That shook him. "Do you really want to kill us all?"

"I'm already going to hell. It'll be a slow bus ride there. Wouldn't mind the company."

"Are you insane?" he nearly shouted.

"Sometimes I wish I was," I nearly laughed. I was beyond tired from holding the electric charge, trying to build it further. "I *truly* want to walk out of damned cave alive." To see Marcel again. To have his smile fill me with warmth. "But if you're just going to shoot me anyway, then I'm taking you with me."

The static grew, a spark dancing from my copper bracelet to Tall's watch. He yelped and let go, his other hand still holding fast.

"Last call boys." I called out to the guards. "You'd kill for this guy, but are you willing to die for him?"

They all glanced between each other, the fourth guard asking the very reasonable question of, "How do we know you won't kill us anyway?"

"Hey." Boss got indignant, but Gunman grabbed him by the arm and shoved the muzzle of his weapon into his side. Nice to know his self-preservation instincts were stronger than his need for petty revenge.

"Well?" The reasonable one pushed.

I was breathing pretty hard through my mouth, my nose clotted with blood. These men killed Drake, who must have bled out by then. They would kill Ryan given the opportunity. And I had no doubt in my mind Boss was responsible for several deaths, and I'm not just talking about the poor wizards caught off guard by the fake Cobalt Star spell.

My conscious was clear.

FIFTEEN[15]

They were waiting for an answer.

They needed to know they wouldn't be wasting their time letting me go. That killing me wasn't worth the risk. For a moment I wasn't sure how I could convince them. Something told me they simply wouldn't take my word for it.

So I looked their boss right in the eye and spoke the only truth that mattered in that moment. "Because I'm not him."

I've killed out of necessity, not entitlement or spite.

But, you know, always a first time for anything.

The men looked between each other as the static charge continued to build. Wordlessly, they came to an agreement and let me go. My arms fell to my sides as I was seriously lacking in the physical strength department, what with all my resources dedicated to keeping a connection to my magic.

Boss started to argue, but the reasonable one took a fistful of his shirt, getting into his face. "You don't pay us enough to fight fucking wizards. They're all fucking insane."

Eh, he's not wrong.

Mr. Reasonable tossed his now ex-employer away, and Gunman batted the man into the ground. That taken care of, the four guards looked to me. I was now the boss.

"Right, guns." I cleared my throat. "Take the clips out. Guns go that way." I gestured with my head. "Bullets that way."

"Magazine," Gunman corrected me as he slid out the *magazine*.

I stared at him blankly. "You know, I'm just gonna let you have that one. Now, anybody got cuffs?"

It was Tall who tossed his gun and then pulled some zip ties from a pocket on his tactical vest.

"That'll work." I took a breath and pushed up off my knees. It nearly killed me, but I needed to keep showing strength and dominance in front of them. I looked back at the Avebury stone and came up with probably my only good idea of the day. "See that big rock? You're gonna play ring-around-the-rosie with it."

Gunman reached down and grabbed ex-Boss by the back of the neck—you know, I never got any of their names. As they all walked over to the stone, Mr. Reasonable asked, "You're not going to leave us here?"

"Not long enough to matter." I was being honest. "Just a little insurance until I can get help. You're going to have to answer to someone much more important than me. I recommend copping a plea deal. The dragons are going to want flesh."

"Dragons?"

"Yeah, you killed one of their golden boys."

Mr. Reasonable looked a little pained, then glanced over at ex-Boss who realized he was going to become a sacrificial lamb, literally. He tried to get away but Vice knocked his head into the stone and that took the fight out of him.

Within minutes the men were standing around the obelisk, their wrists bound together, except for the last one. I carefully took care of that myself. I walked the circle to ensure they had followed my directions and everyone was securely tied off. I couldn't have been more relieved that these men were as smart and self-protective as I had hoped.

I don't want to think about how far I might have actually been willing to go if they put up a fight.

I stumbled back, knocking into a flat display case with a glass top. I doubled over and let go of my magic, driving the electricity into the dirt with a cackling sound as little sparks danced between the folds of my clothes and wisps of my hair.

"Right, that sucked," I said as I got my breath back, my body feeling like jelly.

"You weren't really going to do it, where you?" Mr. Reasonable asked, a bit late of him to do so.

"I'm not known for making good decisions. Ask anyone who's ever met me."

I left them to chew on that little bit of information and started walking towards the tunnel. I made it to the second to last aisle before the entrance. This would be the Anubis aisle, the statue looming ever-present at the far end. Drake's body lay where he fell. As I walked towards him, I might have shed a tear and said a prayer under my breath. He may have deserved a good punch in the face, but not this.

I didn't know why I was going to him instead of straight up to Ryan. It's not like I could drag his body to the surface with me. I'd have to wait until help came. But I couldn't bear the thought of Drake lying there in that dingy place with his eyes open, staring into ugly rock.

His eyes were closed.

"Drake?"

I kneeled down next to his blood-soaked body. The red glistened as if it was full of gold dust. I poked at his chest and he moaned, his head lolling to the side for a moment.

"Holy shit, you're alive!"

"Barely." His eyes opened, slightly glassed over.

"There's so much blood," I stated the obvious, not entirely sure what I should do. I mean, I could put pressure on the wound but if he hadn't bled out by now…

Drake let out a rough laugh. "Human heart adjacent."

I laughed because I could. "You're half-cockroach, Drake."

"On my father's side, I assure you," he joked, or maybe he was delirious. Either way, he was alive. "I need my magic."

"Right, let's get you out of here." I had no idea how to do that. "Can you walk if you use me as a crutch? I don't think I have the strength to throw you over my shoulder."

"I can try." He put his hands flat on the ground and attempted to set up.

Moving behind him, I put my hands on Drake's back and pushed him into a sitting position. He winced and groaned in pain, but if anything, that shot adrenaline through him that helped get him to his feet. I threw his left arm around my shoulder and let him lean on me. Slowly we half-walked, half-dragged our way towards the entrance.

Before we exited, I glanced back to the guards just barely visible in the distance. Still tied together, they watched me intently as I helped Drake, the man they shot and left for dead. I flipped them the bird.

A few steps later and we were finally past the boundary of the magical dampening field. We both took a moment to gather ourselves. I pulled energy in at a rapid pace, dimming the lights for a second. I then infused it into my aching muscles, well, metaphysically speaking. I still wasn't running at a hundred percent, but at least I wasn't going to break down.

"You doing okay over there?" I asked Drake. I could feel his magic swirling around him.

"Getting there," he spoke through gritted teeth.

"Works for me."

We continued down the tunnel, running into Ryan's force field. It was a dirty cantrip. It only really worked against non-wizards because it was very simple and not all that sturdy. Just a little tap and it crashed down. It had served its purpose.

The death-trap escalator was still running. Ryan hadn't bothered to stop it on his way up. I was just glad his magic didn't short out the electrical system. We waddled over to the control panel, hitting stop just as a plate came up to the platform.

"Hey, Drake, think you can ride this thing?"

"Hhmmm?" He was groggy, eyes closed, trying not to die.

"Right. Come on." I walked us onto the platform. Gingerly unwrapping his arm from around my shoulder, I moved him forward, hoping that he wouldn't fall between the platform and plate. His body lurched awkwardly, grasping for the hand hold.

I frowned. "Yeah, that's not gonna work."

Drake was going to fall the moment the machine turned back on. I stepped up, wrapping one hand around his that held the handhold, the other around his waist. My feet were dangling half-off the plate, and I'm pretty sure I was more frightened in that moment than when I wasn't sure I would make it out of the cave alive.

The control panel was a simple electrical system. I made the on-button trip with the proper application of electrical energy. The machine lurched upwards. Drake collapsed against the conveyor and I kept him upright. We were a miserable looking pair as we slowly ascended, the light near fading out into darkness before brightening again.

We reached the top and I tripped the power, stopping us just above the platform. Carefully I stepped Drake off the plate, and nearly tripped.

"Damn, you're heavy," I told Drake as I hauled him into a standing position. "Are you as dense as gold, too?"

"If I were, my dear, you would not be able to lift me," his voice was starting to get stronger and more pedantic, which was a relief.

We trudged along, following the half-buried tracks through the winding tunnel. A cold draft blew past us, whistling eerily. Boss and his men had opened the large bay doors to the building, parking an SUV just a few feet from the mine entrance.

"Ryan?" I called out when I didn't immediately see him.

"Minni?" Ryan's head popped out from behind one of the machines. He took one look at both of us and said, "Holy fuck, are you okay?"

"Hey, language." It sounded funnier in my head. "Block the entrance in case the guys get free and want to reneg on our deal."

"Right." Ryan came out of hiding and walked towards us, giving us a critical eye. "I sent up a flare. If there's a coven within a hundred miles, they should see it."

"Good job." I meant it.

Now, we don't have to tell Ryan he was the only one meant to make it out of this alive, that Drake and I surviving was only a bonus.

We'll keep that between us, okay?

SIXTEEN[16]

As Ryan went about putting a proper shield on the entrance, I hobbled Drake over to the SUV. It hadn't even occurred to me that there were keys I should have grabbed. The locks were electric, so the right amount of electricity applied to the proper motor… and that's about the extent of my lock picking abilities.

I popped the hatch and let Drake collapse into the back. He rolled onto his side and laid there in the fetal position, very unbecoming of a noble dragon. I should've thought to take a picture, but my hands were covered in blood. My lip had stopped bleeding thankfully, and I un-clotted my nose on a random rag I found lying around.

Um, T.M.I.? Sorry.

Ryan appeared holding a briefcase-sized first aid kit that looked a little dusty. "Here, I saw this with the safety equipment."

"You're a prince." I gestured for him to put it down on the edge of the SUV. I located some large alcohol wipes inside the case and started to clean myself up. I went to toss away the wipe when I saw the same shimmer that covered Drake's shirt, only not as concentrated. "Gross," I lamented. "I hope you don't have any diseases, Drake."

He didn't answer, just laid there, intent on his spell work.

Ryan poked at Drake who was not at all very appreciative of this. He was also starting to radiate a lot of heat, burning through magic to heal his wound. His blood had dried into a dull brown, the gold shimmer of it a more striking contrast.

This was when we heard the trucks. Two of them, classic Chevy pickups that looked well cared for, with perhaps a new coat of paint. They drove past the open gate, right up to the building. Considering these vehicles were so old they didn't have electronics, I assumed they were the area coven or local ranchers, or both.

Now, the all important question: Did Boss happen to have anyone else on his payroll?

I put myself between the trucks and the SUV. Ryan sat cross-legged next to Drake in the back, basically using Drake as a space heater. The dragon just laid there like he was trying not to die. I wasn't going to count on him as backup.

Pumping magic into my focus bracelet, I watched carefully as men piled out of the cabs. Six in all, bundled up smartly against the weather. They were native and I wanted to trust them, but paranoia is like my middle name. Or one of them. I have enough to spare.

The leader stepped forward and I magically reached out to confirm that yep, wizard.

"I'm Zahn Mathias, of the Bitterroot Salish."

"Minni Masterson, of the Nebraskan Cheyenne, uh, late of New York." Smooth, Minni.

"You sent the distress flare?" he asked.

"We did," I sized up the group.

They were cautious of us, not that I couldn't blame them. I mean, my clothes were still covered in blood. My lip was busted and I'm sure I didn't get everything wiped off. I still had blood and glitter in my hair, which kind of reminded me of my twenty-second birthday.

"Okay, listen," I decided a tactical approach was called for in this situation. "If you work for the rich white douche boat hiding all the artifacts in the mine below, just tell me now so we can skip to the epic wizard battle where I toast you all because I am so done with this all this shit, like, you don't even know."

What? Being utterly antagonist is a legitimate tactic. It just happens to be the only one I'm any good at.

Mathias stared at me blankly for a moment. "Wait, what?"

"There is a cave under us, in the gold mine," I explained and watched his confusion grow. "It's full of stolen artifacts.

Okay, well, the Cobalt Star was bought legitimately but it was stolen from the kobolds originally, so that's debatable."

"There is a cave of artifacts…?" He had such an honest expression of being utterly lost, I was sure he had no idea what I was talking about.

"Are you a medicine man, Mathias?"

That was the first thing that seemed to make sense to him. "Yes, I am."

"Okay, good." I let out a very long breath. "Long story short, some rich asshat and his four henchmen are tied up in a treasure vault down in the gold mine. They've been squirreling away misappropriated artifacts and killing those who get in their way. We came to steal back one piece of jewelry and nearly died for our troubles. So, we would love it if you could help us. I dunno, you have a local magic council of some sort, right?"

"Yes, in Pablo." He was finally on the same page with me. "You said they're tied up in the mine?"

"Yep."

Mathias turned to his men and started to give orders to the effect of 'go down and bring up Boss and his henchmen.' Ryan had to lower the shield first, of course, while I gave directions. But it became obvious they only really needed to follow the blood trail and shuffled foot prints. I told them there was an anti-magic field that they needed to be careful about. I also warned them about the conveyor belt of death, and they just looked at me like I was crazy.

One of the men grabbed an extra down jacket from his pickup. We shoved Ryan into the coat and then him into the cab, keeping the engine and heater running. He did not complain one bit, just stuck his nose in the air vent and sighed contently.

The healer was looking Drake over, seeing if he could help him recover. And with your other men in the mine, that pretty much left you and me to stand around like awkward prom dates.

"Do you want to give me the short story long?" You asked, concern etched in your face. "Tell me exactly why you're covered in blood and your friend over there is recovering from a seemingly fatal gunshot wound?"

"I'm going to say this was my fault, sorta, mostly. Depends on who you talk to. To be honest, I kind of lost track. I'm pretty sure I passed culpability somewhere between not calling 911 and kidnapping a member of the British monarchy."

"… What?"

"At least this time we didn't lose Delaware."

"You lost Delaware?"

"You know what? Don't worry about that, it's not important right now."

SEVENTEEN[17]

Minni and Mathias sat on a large concrete block inside the mine entrance building. By the time she finished her story, Mathias' men had brought up the henchmen and their ex-boss. They marched the very annoyed looking men past Drake who sat on the back of the SUV, legs dangling over the side.

Drake followed them with sharp eyes, but ultimately did nothing. It was a miracle he hadn't decided to set them on fire. Instead, he watched as they were herded into the back of the pickup truck that didn't shelter Ryan.

"We looked for the dampener first," one of Mathias' men told him as he held out a small wooden box. "We shut it off before handling these guys."

"Thanks, Henry." Mathias looked the box over, taking note of the Persian script on the side.

"Was any of that stuff magical?" Minni asked.

"Didn't do a full inventory," Henry said wryly. "But I did feel some ambient magic. There's probably a few magical items, but mostly it's just art and jewelry."

Mathias handed the Persian box back to Henry. "Alright, get them to Pablo before they freeze to death out here."

"And before Drake decides to take his revenge," Minni added helpfully.

"We'll have the council figure out what to do with them," Mathias said, ignoring her.

"Seeya back there." Henry nodded and headed over to the truck, gesturing orders.

One of the Bitterroot Salish climbed into the back with ex-Boss and the men. A second man jumped into the passenger's seat as Henry got behind the wheel. He threw the truck into reverse and backed out of the complex, speeding off towards the nearest road.

Ryan was watching from the cab of the other Chevy. He turned to Minni to give her a thumbs up. She returned the gesture and looked towards the tunnel. "What are you going to do with it all?"

"Make sure it is returned to its rightful owners," Mathias answered simply.

"Right, sorry." Minni shook her head and rocked slightly. "I think my brain is sherbet now."

"You have been through a major ordeal," he pointed out.

"Is that why I feel like I'm going to throw up?" Minni gave a sad little laugh. "I'm fine, this isn't the worse I've ever had it."

"You mind if I make a personal observation?"

Minni glanced over at the medicine man and considered his question. She was tired, the chemicals that flooded her body during her near-death experience having washed out as she told her story. At this point, she wasn't sure if a lack of caring or a kind of morbid curiosity, led her to say, "Sure, go right ahead."

"You seem a bit lost."

Minni snorted. "What gave it away?"

He ignored her flippancy. "I mean it in every sense, Minni. Every part of you can't seem to decide which side of the river it wants to be on."

"No one has their life completely figured out," she argued, doing nothing to stop Mathias continuing his observation of her.

"At least most people generally know where they want to be," he countered, sounding ever much the concerned leader, like Phil. "You're content to be miserable drowning in the middle."

Minni wanted to tell him that wasn't true. "My entire life, I've always been half of everything. Half-Cheyenne, Half-Irish, Half-a-Witch, Half-Normal, Half-Ignored, Half-Useful, Half-a-Good-Person, Half... of a not so Good Person. Marcel is the closest to making me feel whole, and I half-ass my relationship with him. I think some of us are just meant to be in the middle."

"I'm truly sorry you feel that way."

"You and me both," she replied with a resigned slump of her shoulders. "Anyway, thank you for your help on this. Clean up duty isn't exactly a glamorous job."

"This man has been operating on our land, under our noses, taking these artifacts from other peoples." Mathias smiled. "It will be our pleasure."

"You're an alright guy." Minni gave him a light tap on the shoulder.

He was quite for a moment, as if he was going to continue on with his earlier comments. But he looked her in the eyes, read the room, and instead he asked, "What are you going to do with the Cobalt Star?"

Minni looked to the truck where Ryan sat, the necklace still tucked in his pocket. "I think my first concern is how we're getting back to New York and Wales."

"Lou can walk through shadows." Mathias gestured to one of his men standing by the SUV, chatting. "It's his gift. He can get you wherever you need to be."

"Oh, well, that takes care of that then. Thanks." Minni stood up, the blood on her shirt dry and stiff. "If Drake is ready to travel, then probably best we get back as soon as possible. I haven't heard from Phil or Harper and that worries me a little."

"Let's go check on your friend then."

"I wouldn't call Drake a friend."

"Then what?"

Minni stopped to think about that. "Frenemy, I guess."

She gestured to Ryan, requesting him to come join them before Mathias could continue that topic of conversation. When they reached Drake, the man was still sitting on the edge of the SUV, bloody and disheveled.

"You're right," Minni told Drake. "We really need to stop meeting like this."

Drake let out a tired laugh. "It seems we are even now. I saved your life, and you saved mine."

"I really wish you wouldn't play that game with me," Minni sighed. "I still haven't forgiven you for Stacey."

Drake frowned ever so slightly, as if he could feel an actual modicum of regret. "We never did get off on the right foot."

"Your fault."

"I suppose it was," he quietly agreed.

"Why is it so cold out here?" Ryan asked, shaking already.

"It's the mountains," Mathias said. "Cold air gets sucked down from Canada, plus wind chills and cloud cover keep it from warming up."

"I was not expecting a legitimate answer," Ryan admitted. "But that's cool. And cold."

Mathias lightly chuckled. "Just be glad it's not raining."

"I would die."

"I wouldn't let that happen," Minni said quickly and easily as she held out her hand. "The Star, please."

"Right." Ryan unzipped the front of his borrowed jacket so he could get to the coat Minni loaned him. He was in four layers of clothing and still appeared to be freezing. And there was Minni and Drake, in nothing but bloody shirts and pants, with everyone else bundled against the cold. "Here you go."

Minni took the Cobalt Star from Ryan. This was the first time she had gotten a good look at the gem. It was beautiful, of course, just like its twin. The blue color was vibrant and struck through with the veins of titanium dioxide that gave the sapphire its star.

"It's not magical," Minni declared after sending some magic into it, only to encounter nothing.

"Always a pleasure to be vindicated," Drake said.

"But it is beautiful." The Star sparkled in the light as she rolled it slightly in her hand. She could see why the kobolds would covet it so. The deep, cobalt color was mesmerizing, like an infinite abyss of sky and sea. And while the Star wasn't magical in its own right, it did represent unquestionable power in the value Avalbane had placed on it.

Minni could have the world for the low, low price of the mineral-laced chunk of corundum in her hand.

"Minni?" Mathias said and her head snapped up.

"Hey, Lou." Minni got the shadow walker's attention as she pulled her phone out of her pocket. She quickly brought up a map and showed him the screen. "Can you take us there?"

"Easy," Lou answered.

"Thanks." She tucked her phone away and once again looked into the depths of the Cobalt Star. "Then unless anyone says different, I think it's time we got out of here."

"Take care of what you need to do," Mathias told her. "We will see to the vault."

"Keep me apprised, will you?"

"Of course."

"Oh, and be careful of that Anubis statue. Something ain't right about it."

Mathias chuckled lightly. "We will. Safe travels."

"Thank you." Minni accepted his outstretched hand.

"Thank you, sir." Drake offered his hand to Mathias. "To you and yours."

"And to yours," Mathias replied.

They finished their thanks and goodbyes, then moved away from the SUV. Lou was a natural shadow walker, his foci a curved and twisted walking stick with distinctive marks Minni couldn't recognize. Lou tapped the ground, letting the stick slide up through his loose grip. Then grabbing the foci by the bottom section, he reached forward and tapped the air. A small sliver of nothing appeared, a bend in space doubling as an optical illusion.

Lou walked through first, ensuring that the connection to the Shadow Realm was complete and strong. Minni gestured to Ryan who followed first, disappearing into the nothingness.

"You know what you're doing?" Drake asked, stepping up to the gate.

"Not usually," Minni admitted. "But whatever it is seems to be working for me."

"Yes," he replied, then stepped through the tear.

Minni glanced down at the Cobalt Star, a ticket to having everything she wanted.

But nothing she needed.

Walking through the gate, Minni was met with more cold and a darkened sky. Lamp posts illuminated the soft layer of snow blanketing the rocky landscape. A path was cut into gray stone, sloping down towards a dark wood shed built straight into the rock. Over the double door of the shed hung a plaque with two, crossed pick-axes emblazoned in worn golden paint. Above and below the symbol were the words Clara Stoll.

"Effing hell," Ryan was lightly bouncing on his feet. "You had to go someplace colder?"

"Yeah, I didn't think that part through," Minni said as she reached out and touched his shoulder, sending another wave of thermal energy. Norway, in November, was well below freezing. "We won't be long."

Minni walked down the path towards the door, snow crunching lightly under her feet.

"Where are we?" Ryan asked, pulling his hoody back up.

"The Blaafarveværket," Drake correctly pronounced the Norwegian word. He started to follow Minni. "You're giving the Star back to the kobolds?"

"That's the plan," Minni mumbled.

The wooden double doors to the Clara Stoll mine creaked and opened slightly. Minni and Drake stopped, waiting to see if this was a precursor to another attack. The left side door opened a little wider, and three little goblin heads poked out, their faces knobby and weathered. They started to talk quickly among themselves, eyes fixed on the star sapphire in Minni's hand.

Minni pulled her phone out before kneeling, one knee in the snow, jeans soaking up the water. The Cobalt Star dangled from her fingers precariously as she opened a translation app.

"I am returning the Cobalt Star. It belongs to you," she wrote into the translate field, then hit the *Listen* icon. The computerized voice choppily spoke the phrase in Norwegian, Minni hoping it worked like it was supposed to.

The kobolds stopped talking among themselves and stared at her. She clicked the icon again, holding the phone towards them. One of the kobolds got brave enough to step out from behind the door. His shoeless feet weren't bothered by the snow crunching beneath his toes.

"You're the little guy from the car," Minni said when the kobold got closer. He wasn't mad at her like the pixies had been, but then the lightning bolt hadn't been directed at him.

"*I stopped the pixies,*" Minni quickly tapped into the phone and let the computer speak for her. It was a half-truth. She had been there when the pixies were chomped on and lit on fire.

Little Sweater Guy walked forward hesitantly. When he was close enough, Minni held out the Cobalt Star to him. He reached forward and snatched it from her fingers, nearly taking a pinky with it. Minni wasn't going to be mad at the kobold for being cautious and untrustworthy. He eyed the Star, flipping it around in his hands and holding it up to the moonlight.

"*I recommend better security measures,*" Minni said via the translation app. "*Maybe some spell blocking wards.*"

The kobold glanced up at her, tilting his head in light bemusement.

"Your phone said *spellbreaking departments,*" Drake offered.

Minni looked over her shoulder. "You speak Norwegian? Nevermind, of course you do. You could have said something."

"You should have assumed." Drake smiled. "It also said pixels earlier, instead of pixies. I think the kobolds got the point."

"Useless," Minni groaned, darkening her phone and sliding it into her pocket. Turning her attention back to Sweater Guy, she found him running away from her, disappearing into the mine without so much as a thank you. "How do you say 'you're welcome' in Norwegian?"

"The polite way or the sarcastic way?" Drake asked and both Ryan and Lou snickered.

"Have I mentioned I hate you?" she deadpanned.

"Maybe... I think. It's been a very busy day."

"No kidding."

Minni was tired, and she wouldn't blame herself for it after the day she had. She took a deep breath and pressed her hand into her leg in preparation to stand. That's when the doors of the Clara

Stoll burst open, a wave of kobolds running out like a herd of hellbent goblins.

If she hadn't been as tired as she was, she might have fried them before they even reached her, but she was far too sluggish for that. Minni was overrun by the kobolds who knocked her down like overzealous puppies. She was absorbed into a general group hug with a few kisses placed on the top of her head. And then they were gone, returning to the mine.

Laying on her back in the snow, staring up at the beautiful night sky, Minni was thoroughly bewildered. She saw the faces of Drake, Ryan, and Lou peer down at her, making sure she was okay.

"What just happened?" Minni asked dumbly.

"Seems you've gained the favor of the kobolds." Drake held out his hand. "Avalbane did place a high value on it."

"Oh, great." Minni took the offered hand and let Drake help her stand. That's when she noticed the chunk of dingy silver-colored ore which had been placed in her other hand by the kobolds. "What is this?"

"Cobalt ore," Drake answered.

"I thought cobalt was blue?" Ryan asked.

"Same," Minni added, examining the golf ball sized rock.

"Chemistry, oxides," Drake said lazily. "I could explain but I fear Mr. Thompson here will simply complain about the cold again."

"He's really annoying when he's right." Ryan frowned.

"It was unfortunate Aureolin wasn't at the party," Drake mused. "I would have liked to have seen the look on Minni's face when introduced to a cobalt dragon with yellow hair and olive green skin."

Lou leaned over at Ryan. "Is this normal for you guys?"

Ryan snorted. "What, teaming up with asshole dragons to return stolen non-magical artifacts that magically appeared and disappeared through the centuries?"

"Something like that..."

"I am right here," Drake pointed out.

"On Wednesdays we have book club." Ryan explained further. "We've only accidentally summoned three demons so far."

"Alright." Minni loudly got their attention, too many questions rolling about in her head. It wasn't a feeling she particularly enjoyed, especially when she wasn't even close to knowing any of the answers. "Let's take Drake home next. Then Ryan, you and I need to get back to Brooklyn. We still have an attempted murder to solve."

EIGHTEEN[18]

"Still cold," Ryan said emphatically.

"We'll go to the Mercury Shop next," Minni promised as they stood on the patio outside of Drake's manor house in Wales.

"Well, Miss Masterson." Drake placed his hand over his heart-adjacent and slightly bowed his head. "Always a pleasure, but we really do need to stop meeting like this, or else I can only assume you are a harbinger of doom."

"Not a bad gig if you can get it." Minni shrugged.

The French doors opened and Nev stepped out. The silver dragon took one look at Drake's bloody shirt and crossed her arms in annoyance. "I assume the other individual has been thoroughly dismembered."

"They were carted away before I had the chance," Drake explained with a slight irritant tone to his voice.

Minni realized that wasn't strictly speaking the truth. Drake was more than enough healed to have done damage to the men, set them on fire at the very least. But he hadn't, and for the life of her she couldn't figure out why. It seemed very... non-dragon-like.

Drake turned to Lou. "I'm sure the Bitterroot Salish are more than capable of enacting proper justice. Otherwise the matter can be revisited."

Lou raised a brow at this, judging Drake critically. "That sounded like a veiled threat."

"He does that a lot," Minni said. "Don't worry about it."

Nev made a hrm sound, tightening her jaw as she stared at Drake. He saw this and attempted to ignore her.

Lucy walked out of the house with two totes in her hands.

"Oh!" Minni moved forward. "I forgot about those."

"You got swag bags?" Ryan asked.

"Clothes I'm stealing from Nev here," she explained as she grabbed the totes from Lucy. "I'm gonna give them to Stacey and tell her I got them off eBay."

"Oh, cool, cool." Ryan nodded.

"It's hardly stealing if I give them to you," Nev tsked.

"I think it is time you got home, Miss Masterson," Drake quickly said, exhaustion clearly evident in his tone.

"You know what, Drake, you are right," Minni agreed, moving away to join Ryan and Lou. "If we have to meet again, let's do so in the middle of a desert, alright?"

"I'm sure you'll manage to find the water of an oasis."

Minni dropped her shoulders and said, "Yeah, probably."

"Be well, Miss Masterson," Nev said politely, nodding her head at Minni, then to Ryan. "And you, Mr. Thompson." She looked at Lou to whom she had never been properly introduced. "And I suppose you as well."

"Take nothing dragons say personally." Minni lightly nudged Lou with an elbow. "Let's go, so you can get back home and tell your friends how crazy New Yorkers are."

"Crazy isn't self-aware," Lou pointed out.

Ryan grinned. "I like this guy. He's quiet but fun."

Lou shook his head, and lifted his walking stick, creating another split in the fabric of reality, one that would take them to Brooklyn. He took the first step through, disappearing into the setting sun.

Minni waited for Ryan to take his turn, but before she could move forward, Drake called out her name.

"What?" Minni asked sharply, looking over her shoulder.

"Surely you have noticed you have a natural predilection to protect, Miss Masterson, even at cost to yourself." His words were far too accurate for Minni's liking. "You also have a high tolerance to pain, which serves towards this purpose, but you would still do well to temper your instincts."

Her face broke into a smile. "Then who would save your ass?"

Drake did not find this as amusing as Minni did, and the stern look on his face unnerved her slightly. Minni escaped his gaze through the portal and into the familiar back alley behind the Mercury Shop. The air was crisp, but thankfully not the freezing temperatures that had nearly frozen Ryan to death.

"Thanks for the loan," Ryan said as he pulled off the large down coat he had borrowed.

"You're welcome." Lou threw it over his arm and turned to Minni. "Mathias will be in touch."

"Much appreciated," Minni replied. "You guys take care of yourselves. Let us know if you ever need help. We owe you one."

Lou nodded his agreement, then quietly disappeared.

Ryan was muttering at the back door of the shop before grabbing the handle to push it open. "Don't shoot! It's me!"

"Why can't you knock like everyone else?" Eli shouted.

Following Ryan inside, Minni was greeted by Eli sitting propped up in Ryan's chair, blasting rod held loosely in his hand. Eli had broken his leg back in September while fighting Ignatius Drake and was still healing. But that didn't affect his ability to produce fireballs that could reduce most things to slag. Dragons being a recently learned exception.

"Hey, Eli," Minni said. She tossed the bags beside the sofa where Perkins sat, reading one of Ryan's library books. "What's the word?"

"The gang should be back any minute now," Eli answered. "Last I heard they were heading to the local shadow gate."

Minni frowned, unsure what to do next. She wanted to leave, go to Marcel, but something insider her also wanted to stick around and learn what Phil had found out. Plus, she was covered in bruises and blood, and her lip was busted. She had yet to think of a convincing lie to tell Marcel.

"What happened to you?" Eli asked.

"Got into a fist fight with some rich guy's henchmen."

"This doesn't surprise me."

Perkins had put his book down and sat up expectantly. "Did you find the Cobalt Star?"

"Yes, actually," Minni spoke as if that was the only reasonable thing to have happened in the last forty-eight hours. "I gave it to the kobolds."

"You… what?" Perkins was more confused than anything.

"I know you thought it was your golden ticket, man." Minni could only muster a modicrum of sympathy for him. "Trust me, I did you favor."

Perkins blanched at that and sunk into the sofa.

There was a tap on Minni's shoulder, and Ryan said, "You promised to buy me hot chocolate."

"Oh, right," she looked down at herself. "It will have to be a bit. I'm not going to Dunkin looking like I just got jettisoned from a roller derby."

"This is New York."

Minni was stuck processing if she could, or should, agree with him when there was a knock on the back door. "Hold that thought," Minni told Ryan then went to look through the wide-angle peephole. Satisfied with what she saw, she opened the door and let the group in: Phil with Harper and Vivian in tow.

"What happened to you?" Phil asked the moment he saw Minni with her blood-soaked clothing.

"Dragons," Minni answered simply. "Apparently we're bad for each other's health."

"No kidding. You're a walking biohazard." Phil put his bag down on the table. He paused before asking, "Is Drake okay?"

"Yeah, he's fine," she told Phil, moving towards the stairs. "I'm going to borrow a shirt and clean up."

"Hold a second," Phil said. "Do you have the Star?"

"Oh. No, I gave it to the kobolds."

"You…" he trailed off. "That was probably the best move, as long as they don't lose it again."

"Don't worry, I told them they should work on upgrading their spellbreaking departments, especially against pixels."

Her comment was met with silence.

"It was a whole thing," Ryan explained to the many blank faces. "Don't worry about it."

"The kobolds gave me a shiny rock." Minni pulled the chunk of cobalt out of her pocket for them to see.

Harper was pinching his sinuses, muttering, "*Wizards…*"

"Who had the Star?" Phil asked.

"Some rich white douche," Minni said, then stalled. "Yeah, probably should have gotten his name."

"He had a whole treasure trove of pretties," Ryan added, his voice appreciative until it dropped into disgust. "His dad put the fake spell out there to keep people from getting to the Star."

Phil looked between Minni and Ryan. "Did this guy know about Perkins, or me?"

"Nope," Minni answered. "I doubt he thought twice about the Star for years until we broke into his mine vault."

"Wait, mind vault?"

"Miiiiiiinnnnnnnnneeeee," Ryan said slowly. "Gold mine to be specific."

"Mathias is taking care of it," Minni assured Phil with a wave of her hand. "We should probably send him a gift basket or something."

Phil looked thoroughly confused. "Who's Mathias?"

"Local medicine man," Minni explained. "Nice guy. You'd get along with him."

"Okay." Harper cleared his throat. "As much as I want to know more about what you've been up to, what I'm hearing is that the Star is now out of the equation. I think we need to focus on the fact we still don't know who is after Perkins, as it now seems it wasn't the current owner."

Vivian leaned against the bookcase. "If it was someone also going after the Star, then they don't have any more reason to go after Perkins."

"I'm not sure it was about the Star," Phil replied.

"What?" Perkins sat up almost comically. "I though this whole thing was about getting the Cobalt Star."

"We know who tried to kill you," Phil said bluntly. "It was Francis Cuellar."

"Francis?" Perkins said in utter disbelief.

"That's the Delaware wizard, right?" Ryan asked. "The one you went to for help performing the spell? But he said no?"

"Yeah…" A flash of emotions flickered across Perkins' face. "So, this is about the Star? He wanted it for himself?"

"No," Phil said. "He was just a means to an end."

"More like a hit-man," Harper casually added.

"Okay." Minni sat down on the steps of the stairwell. "Now I think it's your turn to explain."

"Francis owed a demon," Phil started. "It came to collect and was very specific in its commands. Told Francis who, what, when, and how to poison Perkins."

"Seriously?" Ryan asked.

Phil gave a little defeated shrug. "He showed us his notes and everything. The demon said that if he followed everything to the letter, then Perkins's would likely not die."

"*Likely* not die?" Perkins squeaked.

"I got the demon's name," Phil tried to calm him. "I'll do some research, then we'll do a summoning and see if we can't figure this out."

"Good luck with that." Minni slapped her hands on her knees and stood. "Now, I have almost drowned, been attacked by pixies *twice*, and had my nose nearly broken by some very merc-y mercs. I'm going home and going to bed." She turned and looked up the stairs. "After I wash up."

"Hey," Ryan called out to Minni. "You never explained the kidnapping."

"Kidnapping?" Phil asked.

Minni ignored them and plodded up the steps.

In Ryan's bathroom, she cleaned her face, hands, and neck, making sure not to leave a bloody mess as that would be terribly rude. Her lip had stopped bleeding, a shimmering scab forming. Her arms were bruised where the men had held her. Glitter stubbornly clung to her hair. She couldn't go see Marcel like this.

Grabbing a spare shirt, Minni at least looked presentable enough to walk home. That is, she would get some odd looks, but no one would call 911 on her.

Staring at herself in the mirror, she gripped the edges of the sink tightly as she started to crash from the adrenaline highs that had kept her going. Taking deep, measured breaths, she resisted the urge to use magic to perk herself back up. Magic broke the laws of nature, and those laws were there for a reason.

Walking back downstairs, everyone was talking and chatting about whatever else.

"Where's Phil?" Minni asked, not seeing him.

"The front," Vivian answered.

"Kay. I'll, uh, see you guys later." She gave an awkward wave. "And Ryan, I owe you a hot chocolate. I won't forget."

"See that you don't," he replied playfully.

Minni chuckled softly then walked into the front of the shop. Phil stood at the herbs, picking through the tins.

"I'm heading home," Minni said as she approached. "I doubt you'll need me, but if you do, I'll keep my sender on me."

"Thanks for all your help." Phil turned to her, a slightly sad expression on his face. "Ryan filled me in on what you guys were up to. Though I think I'd like to hear the story of what really happened once he left you in the mine, and not what you told him."

Minni tucked her hands in her pockets, shrugging her shoulders. "Why would I lie to Ryan?"

"Because he's a kid," Phil replied easily, "and you're not known for your self-preservation skills. Your instincts, well, there's no good to way to say it, but they're troublesome. It's why you're here."

"Drake said similar." There was a touch of annoyance in her voice.

"He's a smart man," Phil came to the dragon's defense. "Annoying, smug, insufferable, but smart."

Minni rubbed her forehead and gave a defeated sigh. "I just want to go home and take a nap."

"I'm not going to stop you," he replied softly.

"Good." Minni took a deep breath, clearing her head. "You know, it hasn't really hit Ryan what happened, but it will."

"I'm keeping an eye on him," Phil assured her. "Ryan is stronger than most."

"Strength only means you survive the hit." Minni glanced towards the back room. "Doesn't mean it won't knock you down and make you bleed."

"You would know."

"And not a day goes by I wish I didn't," Minni mumbled. "Anyway. I'll see you later. Take care."

"Yeah, go. Get some rest." He almost said as a command. "I'll let you out."

Minni exited through the front door this time, being simpler than going around the building from the back alley. It was after midday, heading towards evening (at least in this time-zone), and the air was crisp. It hadn't snowed yet, but it wouldn't be long before even Minni complained about the cold.

She got to the subway just in time to meet the F train, her MetroCard nearly glued to her license in her back pocket. It wasn't very crowded and no one seemed to pay her any heed. She was staring down at her phone, the latest text Marcel had sent her. She didn't know what she was going to say, other than maybe apologize for being such a disappointment.

The train doors opened and she waited for a handful of people to shuffle off before making her way forward. As soon as she stepped from the platform, one foot on the tacky laminate flooring of the train, there was a flash of light nearly invisible to all others but blinding to Minni. She stumbled forward, right into a glitter-dust devil that swept around her.

"Really?!" Minni angrily shouted through gritted teeth.

Before her was the plum tree-lined path that would take her to Avalbane, branches waving slightly in the wind. The white flowers were shaken from their homes to drift along the glitter-burdened air. It was quite lovely, inasmuch as it was frustrating.

"There has got to be an anti-fae-travel spell out there," Minni mumbled as she dutifully started down the path.

"Oh, there is one." Avalbane blinked into appearance in front of Minni who skidded backwards on the loose dirt. "But you have to inscribe it to your bones and I've been told that is very inconvenient for mortals."

"I gave the Cobalt Star to the kobolds," Minni didn't bother to play at niceties; she was far too tired. "So if you're going to turn me into a toadstool, just do it already."

Avalbane frowned. "You... want to be turned into a toadstool?"

"Not particularly."

"What odd creatures, you mortals." Avalbane tsked, then grabbed Minni by the left arm, intertwining it with hers so they could walk side by side. "So glad you can follow directions."

"I said I gave it to the kobolds," Minni clarified as Avalbane started to move them forward. Minni had apparently not restocked her sense of self-preservation. "You're not getting the Star, not from me anyway."

"And that's perfect!" Avalbane squeezed up against Minni like they were now best friends. "Everyone followed their script perfectly. Well, almost everyone. Shame about the pixies, but honestly, crashing a gathering of large, lizard-bird... things... Not a very wise decision."

"I'm... really confused." Minni stopped them, trying to excavate her arm from Avalbane's. "And I kinda want to stay that way. Can I go home?"

"But I'm just so ecstatic, I have to tell someone." Avalbane moved back in front of Minni, clasping her hands under chin, her ombre hair sparkling as it waved in the wind. "I've been planning this for years, ever since you were brought to my attention after blacking out that city."

Minni frowned. "New York? Don't you mean weeks?"

"Possibly," Avalbane shrugged then giggled. "Fall off the Arrow of Time once or twice and it's all just relative."

"That... does not sound good for your health."

"I know." Avalbane smiled gleefully. "But that, my dear, is an entirely different tale and we have far too little time as it is."

"Does this mean I can go?" Minni said hopefully.

"Yes, yes, in a moment," Avalbane waved her off and

started walking down the path, her hair and dress moving with the wind as if it was a part of it, rather than being affected by it. "It's as I said. Mortals: you get smarter every century, but you're still as easily manipulated as you're always been."

Minni frowned, following Avalbane for a lack of any better options. Orange blossoms fell from Avalbane's crown and mixed with the petals of the plum trees in the air. They danced on the wind around Minni, sticking to her clothing and gathering in her hair as if they were consciously trying to cling to her.

"You know, I knew where the Cobalt Star was this whole time," Avalbane said casually.

"You... what?" Minni started swiping at the petals but it was like trying to brush off cat hair.

"Just some seemingly useless piece of information I picked up somewhere," Avalbane explained as she stopped and turned to face Minni. "It really needed to go back to the kobolds, but I couldn't be the one to give it to them."

Minni stopped her fruitless effort of trying not to become laden in flowers, looking directly at Avalbane. "You knew I'd give it to the kobolds."

"You do catch on quick." Avalbane's demeanor changed, everything that shone bright sharpened into a razor's edge. It all went gray, and where she was once the wind, she was now the storm. "Of course, you almost ruined everything. You were going to leave the game. A few hours here and you were put right back on track."

"You set this all up..." Minni tried to move away but was constricted by the petals.

Avalbane grinned, fear dripping from her teeth. "Finding that Welshman was like divine inspiration. His family owed a debt to another fae; I'm sure he didn't tell you. But it hardly matters now that it's been repaid."

Minni barely heard her as she tried to send out a kinetic shield, or light the damn flora on fire. Nothing worked and Minni began to panic, the sheer dark miasma flowing from Avalbane beginning to leech across her body.

"A shell game of favors and a touch of blue…" Avalbane hummed and looked worried. "I hope it wasn't too much blue. I think it might have been just the right amount."

"What are you doing?" Minni managed to bite out. She was cocooned in the petals, not even standing on her own weight anymore. "Let me go."

"Let you go?" Avalbane laughed, moving forward with all the grace of a typhoon. "And what would you give me in return?"

Orange blossoms tightened around Minni's throat, cutting off her ability to breath. "Nothing."

"Nothing?"

"I haven't drank anything. I haven't eaten anything," Minni's voice was strained. "You can't keep me here. You have to let me go."

Avalbane turned angry, her eyes filled with the shear brutal force of a crashing wave. "You mortals. Always thinking you're so smart. So why don't we change the game? Hmm? What if I plucked every mortal you know and dropped them in a random spot of the Shadow Realm?"

"Don't," Minni cried out, struggling against the flora with renewed vigor. Her own magic felt useless against the fae's.

"Maybe I'll do it anyway." Avalbane's laugh echoed through her. "Maybe it's time the Seelie Court started to take back its place in the world of man."

Minni had no idea why Avalbane had turned like she did, what beef she had against her or wizards in general, and frankly, Minni didn't care. Avalbane was threatening everyone Minni knew, all her friends, family, coworkers, and that's all she needed to know. Every survival instinct Minni had shut down and she became consumed with only one thought: stop the fae, destroy her if you have to.

Letting go of her magic, Minni reached out for Avalbane's. The petals were seeped in fae magic which burned hotter than anything Minni had ever experienced, including Draconic. She grabbed it anyway, building insulating buffers of auric energy to keep herself from spontaneously combusting.

Minni pulled at the fae magic, drawing it into herself, containing it as she would any other. The more she drew away, the weaker the petal cocoon became. A burst of kinetic energy cracked her prison, the petals tumbling through the air in a cascade of white, gathering around Avalbane like angry sea foam.

Exhausted, Minni fell to her knees.

"Perfect," Avalbane said and the storm calmed.

Breathing heavily, Minni tried to get back on her feet, but Avalbane grabbed her chin and forcefully held her face.

"Do not think me so crass as to dissolve into such tactics, little witch." Avalbane smiled sweetly as her nails dug into Minni's cheek. "I only needed to confirm what you are, what you can do."

"What... what are you talking about?"

Avalbane let go and let Minni collapse onto the back of her legs. "I gather knowledge. I gather favors. And I gather *weapons*. Should I need them."

"Need for what?"

"Now, you don't need to know the details, my dear. It's not like you'll remember them."

Avalbane clapped her hands and the world exploded into white, sweeping Minni away on a torrent of wind. When she could breathe again, she was standing in a familiar hallway.

"Marcel...?" Minni mumbled.

A slight note of panic set in as she couldn't remember how she had gotten to her boyfriend's apartment.

Memories slowly sank into place, a varnish that would cover the damage underneath. An image of a smiling Avalbane forgiving Minni, and being far too polite about the situation. Of the fae giving Minni a small parting gift for her troubles.

Minni reached up and touched her lip, the wound gone, skin unbroken. She glanced down at her wrists, the bruises faded away. Her clothes had been replaced, one of her many Purdue t-shirts stolen from her closet.

The door opened and Marcel stepped out, startling only slightly at seeing her. "Hey, I was gonna meet you downstairs."

"Hey," she replied as he leaned in for a hug and a kiss.

"I got your text," he said as he closed his door. "I like the idea of hitting someplace to eat, but I was thinking Thai instead."

"Thai sounds great." Minni did not remember sending any such text. It was clear to Minni that Avalbane was entirely too manipulative for her own good. The fae's actions had to be covering something up. The idea of it practically screamed at her, clawing for an answer she knew was there.

Marcel offered his arm and Minni decided that trying to understand Avalbane's game was a fool's errand. For all she knew, the fae would completely forget about her after a few days. Or she'd wake up one day and discover herself to be a toadstool. Either way, there's nothing she could really do about it now.

"Sorry about the weekend," Minni said as they headed to the stairwell. "It's been a bit of a mess."

"It's alright," he assured her. "You help people, Minni. It's what you do. It's one of your best traits."

"Yeah. Right between my encyclopedic knowledge of the integrated circuit and my ability to roll my tongue."

Marcel looked at her seriously. "I'm going to have to rate your wit low on the list."

"Don't you dare." Minni play punched him lightly in the shoulder.

Laughing, he smiled broadly at her. "I'll revisit the list."

"Yeah, you do that." Minni tried not to smile, failing.

They got to the open stairwell, Marcel asking. "But your friend is okay, right?"

Minni had difficulty answering the question, and not because she would have to make up some lie to cover her magic. She didn't know what would become of Perkins, or if he was still a target. Something told her he was safe now. Maybe it was instinct, maybe just wishful thinking. But she did know that Phil would take care of things, it's what he did.

But she couldn't help but feel like she should be angry.

"It's all good now," she said, feeling fairly certain she lied.

NINETEEN[19]

Sure, it was strange that Avalbane would give a gift without asking for anything in return. But then, Avalbane wasn't listed as a major player, possibly because she was a softy. Except Drake had said this was something she only wanted others to believe. What was the truth?

Minni decided it was one of those 'cross the bridge when she came to it' kind of situations. No point in poking the bear if the bear had an even chance of wandering off, never to return.

That didn't stop her from putting specific anti-fae wards on her apartment and asking Phil to let her know if he found any anti-fae personal spells that didn't require major surgery. Just as a precaution. Seemed like the smartest, albeit only, move she really had.

The only thing Minni worried about at the moment was her job. Coming back on a Monday after a long holiday weekend was the worst. She stared at the schematics for a control system that just wasn't working in the model. She knew where it was failing, but the reason for it was somewhere upstream and she couldn't quite put her finger on it. Her direct supervisor had given her the task of fixing it, today if at all possible, and Minni was in no position to admit defeat.

Two months previous she had been kidnapped by an insane cultist—twice—and left for dead on a rooftop in the fashion district. That was the story her coworkers were told anyway. There were so many eggshells, Minni could have sworn it was Easter already.

Minnie's phone vibrated on silent and she welcomed the distraction. She picked it up and kept her voice low, not wanting to disturb the other engineers in the cubicles beside her. "Yell-o."

"ALL THE CHOCOLATE!" Ryan screamed in her ear.

"What?"

"It came this morning and you would not believe all the chocolate like there is Belgium Bolivian Swiss and countries I'm sure I've never heard of and there are truffles and hot chocolate and all the chocolate."

"Ryan, breath," Minni quickly interjected.

"Sorry, I may have eaten, oh, I dunno, three boxes of truffles waiting for the phone to degauss."

Minni bowed her head, pinching the ridge of her nose. She did not nearly sacrifice herself in a dank gold mine to save Ryan if he was just going to put himself into a diabetic coma. "Where did you get the chocolate?"

"Drake!" Ryan made a noise somewhere between a squeak and a laugh. "He brought me chocolate and tickets to the next Purgatory concert in Jersey as a thank you for my part in retrieving the Cobalt Star and saving his life."

"It's his way of saying he doesn't owe you anything." Minni sighed, thinking of how quickly Drake must have put this together after having only left him in Wales the previous day.

"Yeah, I got that." Ryan didn't seem too terribly bothered.

Minni made a mental note to contact Mathias and see if Drake had been in touch with him as well. Drake had made it very clear he was never one to owe anyone, anything, ever. Especially other magic users. There was also the matter of Drake possibly wanting payback against the men who shot him.

"Is Drake still there?" Minni asked.

"No, he and Phil went off, somewhere. But seriously, this is a shit ton of chocolate. They had to cart it in!"

"Just… drink plenty of water and protein, okay?"

"Chocolate covered hazelnuts and almonds count?"

"Probably not," Minni replied dryly. "Save me some of the Bolivian chocolates?"

"I make no promises," he said dead seriously.

Minni laughed and after a few short words, ended the call. Helping out dragons did seem like a pretty sweet gig, what with remodeling bathrooms, luxury candies, and the not murdering everyone who slightly wronged them. But then, one would have to deal with dragons.

Going back to her work, having the distraction did indeed clear her mind enough that she focused better on the task. Within two hours she had the model running through without failure. She sent an email to her supervisor, letting him know she was finished just in time for a late lunch.

Her phone started to vibrate, this time from an alert. Then it vibrated again, and again. She snatched up the phone before it could vibrate itself off the desk. Stacey had been posting to Twitter so rapidly that the system decided Minni should know.

"This is so amazing, can't even tell you!!! Met the awesome #NicoleNova!" her first tweet said, accompanied by a selfie of Stacey and a woman with jet-black hair and fierce eyebrows.

Minni had no idea who Nicole Nova was.

A quick Google search revealed Nicole to be one of the rising stars in Hollywood, at least this week. That night she would be attending the world premiere of the latest Oscar-bait film in which she had a pivotal supporting role.

Minni had never heard of the movie.

As Minni scrolled down through the Twitter chain, a story unfolded of how this actress was in need of something to wear to the premiere and had come across the boutique that Stacey worked in. Nicole loved Stacey's use of colors, how she could make even the brightest of neons work without being gaudy, fluorescent, or horribly retro. It was all about volume and accents.

Minni was pretty sure it was a form of witchcraft she was unfamiliar with.

Scrolling through, there was plenty of photos of the fitting, Stacey having not been able to post them in real time. Minni was happy for her friend, liking everything. She was about to reply to one post when something caught her eye. An extremely familiar hat that she had seen very recently on a specific English princess.

A more in-depth Google search later and her suspicions had been confirmed. Minni got up and walked down the hallway to some empty offices at the far end. It was where everyone went when they didn't want to be overheard by nosey coworkers.

Knowing it was going to cost her, in a literal sense, Minni dialed a number she wasn't even sure why she saved. She was met by an odd double dial-tone rather than the typical long dash. After three of these, he finally picked up.

"Miss Masterson," Drake greeted her.

"Did you call in your chip with Princess Valerie so she'd get her niece to buy one of Stacey's dresses?" Minni didn't bother to be subtle. It was something she had difficulty with anyway.

"Of course not," Drake replied, insulted. "All I did was get an up-in-coming actress in a store, anything after that was left purely up to Miss Sanchez."

Minni stumbled for a second, then blurted out. "Why are you doing this?"

"It seemed like the best way to compensate Miss Sanchez for performing unwanted magical spells on her," Drake explained as if it was the most obvious of conclusions.

"You never cared before," Minni pointed out.

"To be honest, I don't terribly care right now," Drake replied candidly. "Miss Sanchez is of no concern to me, but she is a concern to you. I hope that this gesture will open a friendly dialogue between us, or at least end you threatening to hit me every five minutes."

"I… I have no words for you right now." Minni clearly did not mean this in a good way.

Drake chuckled anyway. "I am simply attempting to make peace, Miss Masterson. You are of much more value to me as… a friend."

While he might have thought he was being cute or genuine, Minni became incensed. She knew what he meant, what they always mean. She was more valuable as an asset.

That's why she was shuffled off to New York instead of imprisoned by the council for performing a Black Listed spell. They wanted to keep her handy in case they had use of her against the TechnoMages. It was why she met Drake. Phil knew

Minni would be handy to him as a magic sink and asked her to tag along to investigate Canton back in September. Minni got her second job as a tour guide because one entrepreneurial woman realized just how useful Minni could be to the tourist industry.

Minni had pretty much accepted it as part of her life. But today, being reminded of her standing in the magic community as little more than a useful tool, it bled like a fresh wound.

"This thing that you did, it wasn't for me," she told Drake coldly. "It was for Stacey because even though she didn't know it, you owed her. Big. Just be glad this didn't backfire in your face."

"I did my research—"

"Yeah, I don't care," she snapped at him. "If you had really wanted to make nice, to try to become friends or whatever, then you would have come to me first about wanting to make it up to Stacey."

There was a slight pause. "You're upset."

Minni let out a strangled laugh. "He *can* be taught."

"I'm going to close this conversation, Miss Masterson," he replied with some dignity, "as it is clear this is not a good time."

"Yeah, you're right," she said with a regretful sigh. "If I ever hear from you again, Drake, something better be on fire... Wait... frozen solid? Whatever, you get the point."

"Indeed I do. Good day, Miss Masterson."

Drake hung up on Minni before she could. A small part of her regretted speaking so harshly to him. She put her phone down on an empty desk and rubbed at her temples, feeling like she was standing slightly off kilter, forgetting something important.

Minni's phone beeped again, this time a text from Stacey.

"*OMG! I'm making a dress for a red carpet event!!!!!!!!!!!!!!! [three heart emojis].*"

"*I saw!! That's amazing!!*" Minni replied.

"*I have so much last minute tailoring to do. I'm shaking!*"

"*You'll do great. Just remember to breathe.*"

"*Hahahahahahah, no time for breathing, gotta sew [three crying emojis],*" Stacey sent back, then quickly followed up with. "*Red carpet watch party, tonight, Chelsea's.*"

"I'll be there," Minni promised.

Stacey replied with nothing but emojis and that made Minni laugh. She was glad Drake's plan had worked when it could have gone seriously wrong. Minni knew Stacey was talented, but that didn't mean some fly-by-night starlet thought the same.

Minni headed back to her desk, texting Marcel what had happened and that she'd be at Chelsea's probably all night. She returned just in time to hear her work phone go off. She snatched up the receiver. "Masterson."

"This is reception," the other person said. "There's a bike messenger here who has something for you. Bring your ID."

"I'll be right there."

Having no idea why a bike messenger would be delivering anything to her, Minni still grabbed her license and headed to reception. A very impatient looking man stood next to the desk, checking his phone. As soon as he saw her, he perked up and grabbed his clipboard from where it sat on top of a small brown box, no bigger than a lunch bag.

"Dominque Masterson?" he asked her.

"Yeah." Minni tried to eye the label on the box as she handed over the ID.

"Sign here." He placed the clipboard directly in her hands after he confirmed her identity.

Minni signed and he quickly took back the item whilst simultaneously replacing it with the box and ID. He then booked it the hell out of there; onto his next job, Minni assumed. A part of her had the horrible sinking feeling she had just been handed a bomb or something. Her life was pretty crazy as of late.

She was calmer, but no less confused, when she read the return label. It was sent from Pennington-Kettering Enterprises, their New York office. This was Drake's company, although Minni figured it was probably a money laundering front or something.

Drake had sent Ryan chocolate and Stacey a commission, so this was likely along those veins: something to prove beyond doubt that he didn't owe her anything.

With a roll of her eyes, Minni headed back to her cubicle with the box. Upon getting there, she tossed it onto the desk and searched for a pair of scissors. Finding a useful pair on Gary's desk, Minni went about cutting the tape and opening the parcel. Several packing peanuts tried to explode out, clinging to the lid. A quick tug at the static buildup and they dropped, no longer electrically charged.

Minni reached in to find an engraved box plated in copper.

The lid of the box showed a fully armored knight with a dragon, wings flared, behind him. The sides depicted armies, a king, and a book. It was a visual representation of the story of the Copper Knight, Minni would know it anywhere. And the box wasn't new: the copper had become burnished to a shiny brown with years of handling. There were even little specks of green in the deep edges.

For a good five minutes, Minni simply stared at it.

Opening it up, a folded piece of heavy cardstock was immediately visible, laying on top of something uneven. Minni lifted the paper and nearly yelped. Sitting on a specially designed padded rise was the Star of Serendipity.

Minni became almost paralyzed at the sight of it. The starburst ruby was worth more than she was, and she was tossing it around just moments earlier. It was also now in her very unsecured possession, although, why did she even have it in the first place?

Opening the paper, she read the note to herself:

It is very serendipitous that there is no such thing as fate. –
Nevina Argent

Minni sat back in her chair, the cardstock loosely dangling from her fingers. She stared at the Star of Serendipity which oddly reflected the fluorescent lights. Then, louder than was prudent, she muttered, "Now what the fuck is that supposed to mean?"

ABOUT THE AUTHOR

Jessica D. Coplen is a born and raised Oklahoman who loves to travel and learn new things. She received a Bachelor's in History from Northeastern State University in Tahlequah, Oklahoma. She lived in Warwickshire County, England (Tolkien's shire) for several years after college before returning to Oklahoma. Besides writing and travelling, she enjoys reading, carpentry, going to movies, and painting her nails. She's been caffeine free since 2010 and it was one of the best decisions she's ever made.

Jessica likes to think of herself as living proof that
life changing events don't have to be all that life changing.

Special Sneak Peek
Book Three

Copper and Mercury

Copper and Mercury

"Minni… have you gone to bed?"

"The cat's been fed," I mumbled, despite the fact that neither my boyfriend, nor myself, own a cat.

"Okay, I need you coherent right now." Phil's voice teetered between anxious and completely done with me.

"Alright, sec." I placed the phone over my chest, focusing. I touched my aura and pulled at the magic, sending energy through my body. Like a jolt of caffeine or a jump scare, I became energized to the point that I was wide awake. I sat up in bed, running my free hand through my hair as I went back to the phone. "Okay, I'm good. You got arrested?"

"Yes." Phil was definitely done with me. "I nearly took down their booking computer so I'd like to get out of here before I cause any real damage."

"Tell me what you need me to do."

"Go by the Mercury Shop," he said as I started to get out of bed. "Ryan knows where I keep the petty cash, there should be enough. You'll need to use the shadow gate near the shop. Use the map; it's like two lefts and a right to get you to Rome."

"Italy?" I almost squeaked.

"Upstate New York." The connection crackled. "Be as quick as you can."

"I'm on it," I assured him but the phone cut off.

I went to the bathroom and considered taking a quick shower. Kind of wish I had. Seeing as I was at Marcel's, I had some clean clothes, just not a large selection. I grabbed yesterday's jeans, but since they're jeans, they're okay. It only took me like five minutes before I was putting on my sneakers.

"You leaving?" Marcel asked, finally joining the land of the living himself.

"Yeah, I have to bail Phil out of jail."

Marcel rolled over. "What was he arrested for?"

"I dunno," I admitted, because I honestly didn't think to ask. "Can't be all that bad, it's only a five-hundred-dollar bail."

"Want me to come with?" He's such a sweetheart.

"Nah, you sleep. You have to be up dog ass early," I reminded him. Marcel's on the Eastern Europe desk all week while one of his coworkers is on vacation. That means a really messed up sleep schedule for him, and me trying to be supportive and all that. "No need for you to suffer, too."

I gave him a kiss, grabbed my stuff, and headed out the door. It was hella cold outside because, well, New York... in February. I'm from Nebraska, and I tell you, it's not natural for some place to be so cold, so often, for so long.

Yes, I know how climates work, that's not the point.

Now, I'm really good at controlling energy: it's my special skill. So it's easy for me to create a thermal shield. It keeps me warm in these kinds of conditions. I don't like to use it in front of Marcel because he might get suspicious of how I'm not freezing to death in this weather. Doesn't stop me from complaining about the cold though. You know, to keep up appearances.

Oh, it had snowed, so that was fun.

I got to the Mercury Shop in decent time after calling ahead to Ryan. I could see him waiting for me when I got to the front of the shop. He quickly unlocked the door and let me in.

"What did Phil get arrested for?" he asked as he locked up.

"I dunno." I shrugged and headed towards the back where the shadow gate maps were kept.

"You didn't ask?"

"Didn't seem relevant at the time." Translation: I never ask these things, which is why I'm always getting myself into trouble.

"Huh," was Ryan's only comment.

I started sifting through all the ledgers that sat on a bottom shelf. Eventually I found the New England book and pulled it out from under half a dozen others. With a thud, I set it on the table and flipped through it to get to the Rs.

"Oh, great. There are two Romes."

"In Italy?"

"No, upstate New York." I pointed at the lines that listed both cities with completely different directions through the Shadow Realm. Who knew there was two of them?

"Rome, New York?" Ryan quietly questioned before making a sudden, "Oh," sound.

"What?"

"Werewolves."

"Werewolves?"

"Werewolves."

"Ugh, *Werewolves*."